HONK
IF YOU
HATE
ME

HONK IF YOU HATE ME

DEBORAH HALVERSON

Delacorte Press

*Thank you to tattoo connoisseur Mary Halverson
and inker extraordinaire Chad Hillix
for their insight and generosity*

Published by Delacorte Press
an imprint of Random House Children's Books
a division of Random House, Inc.
New York

Delacorte Press and colophon are registered trademarks
of Random House, Inc.

www.randomhouse.com/teens

Educators and librarians, for a variety of teaching tools, visit us at
www.randomhouse.com/teachers

Library of Congress Cataloging-in-Publication Data
Halverson, Deborah.
  Honk if you hate me / Deborah Halverson. —1st ed.
    p. cm.
  Summary: Blamed for ruining her town by burning down a factory ten years
earlier, sixteen-year-old Monalisa Kent decides to take charge of her life but is
unprepared for the revelations and revolution that follow.
  ISBN 978-0-385-73393-9 (hc)
  ISBN 978-0-385-90407-0 (glb)
  [1. Self-actualization—Fiction. 2. Guilt—Fiction. 3. Fathers and
daughters—Fiction. 4. Tattooing—Fiction. 5. Fires—Fiction.
6. Depression, Mental—Fiction.] I. Title.
PZ7.H1678Hon 2007
[Fic]—dc22
                                                                            2006023935

The text of this book is set in 11-point Sabon.
Book design byTrish P. Watts
Printed in the United States of America
10 9 8 7 6 5 4 3 2 1
First Edition

For my dad, Patrick,
who told me girls can do anything

For my mom, Marianne,
who showed me girls can do anything

And for my husband, Michael,
who believes this girl can do anything
—D.H.

We're our own dragons as well as our own heroes,
and we have to rescue ourselves from ourselves.

—TOM ROBBINS

PROLOGUE

It was just a picture, a cover photo on a magazine. One small girl, two wide, blue eyes—scared eyes.

I didn't see the photographer. I don't remember what happened.

It was just a picture—but it changed everything.

1

The wrinkled checker kept looking up at me. She'd scan an item, then look up. Scan, then look up. Scan, then . . .

"Hey, aren't you—"

"No." I cut her off.

She didn't say anything else.

Outside the 7-Eleven, when I told Glenn, he asked me what I expected. "Your 'look at me' blue hair attracts attention, Mona." He rummaged through the plastic grocery bag.

"It's 'leave me the hell alone' blue." I snatched the bag and fished the gum from under his Superman comics, taking a piece to stash in the pocket of my cutoffs before handing him the pack. "Anyways, that old lady had blue hair, too."

But it wasn't my hair the woman was interested in. That tottery nosey-body wanted to know if I was That Monalisa Kent Girl.

That's all anyone wanted to know when they saw me. It's why I finally decided to dye my dull brown hair yesterday. Distract them. Make them focus on my blue hair instead of my face. My eyes. The darn things were wider and bluer than Superman's tights.

Using my teeth, I ripped the plastic off the top of a lime Otter Pop, then stepped my beat-up beige work boots onto my skateboard. Glenn lightly pushed the small of my back, and we were off. Holding the Otter Pop above my head with the label facing back at Glenn, I called out, "Sir Isaac Lime says, 'Thank you.'"

"Sir Isaac Lime has manners. You should ask him for lessons."

"Waste of time, Popeye. I yam what I yam."

With his long, floppy strides, Glenn caught up to me within a few feet. He'd pulled his Batman ball cap low over his sunglasses, which were thickly lensed and majorly tinted to protect his damaged optic nerves. He wore them indoors and out. I rested my free hand on his wide shoulder and let him pull me along. All I had to do was enjoy my ice pop and occasionally point out a rock or a piece of litter for Glenn to swerve around. The Pink Cloud was only a few blocks away and we were in no hurry. Summer days were meant to be lived slowly.

While I sucked my icy treat, Glenn popped his Bubble Yum. Four blocks of popping. Truly annoying, but I didn't rag on him about it. Instead I listened closely and realized he was popping out a tune. Impressive. Glenn might be blunderheaded about all things athletic, but everything else, he had wired.

It was only four o'clock when we got there, but since it was Friday, the Pink Cloud was already fully packed and highly adrenalized. Glenn's parents knew exactly what they were doing when they opened their tattoo parlors there—right in the heart of downtown and just two blocks from the university. The Pink Cloud Tattoo Salon dominated one side of the block, facing the park. Dante's Inferno, Ink., backed up to it, on the other side of the block, facing the burned-out plant. Most people had no clue that the same family owned both studios. Most people assumed the shops were in competition. Most people forgot that when you assume things, you make an *ass* of *u* and *me*.

The genius is that the Pink Cloud and Dante's served totally different breeds of tattoo junkie.

Glenn's mom ran the Pink Cloud. It was hip, posh, and pink up the wazoo. Its fuzzy, frilly tattoo chairs made Starbucks-swilling college girls shiver with delight. But then, Margarita Glenn served her own special blend of espresso during inking sessions, so maybe those shivers were caffeine jitters. Whatever their reason, girls wanting their dainty ankles decorated with hearts and flowers swamped the place.

Never one to miss a business opportunity, Margarita had the frat boys covered, too. Black-and-white checkerboard floor tiles and glossy, framed hot-rod posters injected enough testosterone into the Barbie-pink studio to make guys feel secure. Which meant I was happy, too, because even though I usually felt an urge to spew in the presence of girly-girl things like pink suede couches, I truly relished watching trendy boys fight back tears as Margarita needled barbwire tattoos into their biceps and told them how strong and brave they were. Glenn's mom knew how to work the college crowd, all right.

Macho guys who'd rather drink oil coolant than espresso opted for Dante's. Glenn's dad headed that operation. Tucker Glenn's motto was "Tattoos for the Damned," and his customers were hard-core: chains and leather, colors and signs. And everyone who worked there was covered with ink. The newest needle wielder, Chet, even had a bold black tribal design swirled around his left eye, with a wooden peg poked through his eyebrow as a centerpiece. Dante's was cool to its hard-edged core, with its steel-plated walls, medieval-muraled ceiling, pounding speakers, and studly guys. It was my kind of scene all the way—and the only real sign of life in a town that had flat-lined years ago.

Tuck didn't share Margarita's trendy business style. He was a purist. Other tattoo artists might stencil tattoos from mass-market design sheets onto customers who didn't know the difference and didn't care, but Tuck would hack off his own hand before he'd trace the lines of a press-on template. As far as he was concerned, "flash tattoos" were as artistic as bumper stickers. Tuck created his own designs, and tattoo enthusiasts flocked from miles around to have him ink their bodies.

Between the two studios, way in the back, was the Hole, a microscopic back room crammed with a mini fridge, a mini microwave, and a mini TV. More tunnel than room, the Hole allowed me and the Glenns to scuttle between both studios without trudging outside and around the block.

With the Hole being so puny and the Pink Cloud being so pink, Glenn and I hung out at Dante's. Most days, the Inferno stayed mellow until after the sun sank, its customers being the kind who roam mostly after dark. We made Dante's our hangout long ago, back in our smelly diaper days when my dad talked the Glenns into babysitting me while he worked. Now, with me sixteen and Glenn fifteen, we spent all our free time together in Tuck's studio. It helped that Tuck favored comfy futons and furniture made from old car parts, making it a real homey place to kick back. Why shouldn't it be? The Glenns spent most of their time at the studios. Their house was just a place to sleep at night.

I hated that time, when they went home to sleep. It meant I had to go home, too. And my house was anything but homey.

P-tuey! Glenn spit his gum into the trash can, arching it over a bumper-turned-lamp for a three-pointer from the saggy futon.

"Nice technique, bubble boy."

He dipped his head slightly to acknowledge my compliment. The guy was nearly crippled by butterfingers and two humongous left feet, but his lips had better aim than Allen Iverson from the three-point line. Me, I'd only made that shot once. Every other time I had to haul myself off my keister, pluck my chewy wad off the lampshade, then slam-dunk it into the can, Shaquille O'Neal style. Maybe today would be my lucky day.

P-tuey!

Nope. I got up for yet another walk of shame to the lamp.

"Oh, hey"—I spun away from the lamp to face Glenn—"isn't the Guy coming today?"

Glenn shook his hound-dog head and tossed a fresh hunk of Bubble Yum at his mouth. It bounced off his teeth. Invoking the five-second rule, he swiped the sugary cube off the floor and set it directly onto his tongue.

"Nope. Maybe tomorrow." He chewed rapidly. "Or maybe the next day. Can't count on the Guy like a regular person." He tilted his head back and stuck his nose up in the air. His deep voice went all snooty. "He's an *artiste*." *Snap, snap, snap*. More bubbles.

I slam-dunked my gum, then wiped the slobber on my cutoffs. "Shoot, I'm stuck at home tomorrow. I'll miss him again. I gotta see this guy—it's killing me."

"You and everyone else. But it's never gonna happen. He's not into that. It's the art, not the glory." He snapped out "Twinkle, Twinkle, Little Star," or something like it.

Whispered myths about the Guy had swirled in Muessa Junction for years—he gave this boring town something to be excited about. Except for the Glenns, though, nobody had seen him, not even the lucky stiffs he tattooed. He made them wear hoods over their heads as he drilled ink masterpieces into their flesh. It heightened the mystery and the myth—and the reputation of Dante's.

"What's up tomorrow, anyway?" he asked.

I let my body go limp and landed heavy on the futon. "It's the eleventh."

"Oh, that's right." Glenn waved his large hand with a flourish. "The day of glory!" When I made a face, he got serious. "I'm sorry, Mona. I know it sucks." He offered me the last piece of gum, but I pushed it away. "Even Superman has his kryptonite. You'll get through it; you always do."

I sighed dramatically, like I didn't care, then looked around for something else to talk about. Inside, my heart drummed right past "Twinkle, Twinkle, Little Star" and pounded out a heavy-metal drumfest to wake the dead. A half-digested Twinkie threatened a reverse trip up my throat.

It was the same every year. If only I could cut July eleventh right out of the calendar. Would my dad even notice? Of course he would. His annual gloating was his reason for living. He had to celebrate the day he saved Glenn. And me. From me.

And WOPR Local 10 News *loved* its town hero. Like clockwork, they called every July first to set up the taping. Viewers needed their "Where Are They Now?" segment, after all. Heck, without an annual update, they might not know That Monalisa Kent Girl when they saw her. And we couldn't have that happen. How would they know who to aim their bitter stares at?

Actually my dad called the crew this year, a week early. He'd wanted to get a jump on things, this being the tenth anniversary and all—the tenth anniversary of the first day of the end of my life.

A rapid series of snaps jogged me out of my wallowing. "What the heck was that?"

Glenn tried to slurp in the tattered shreds so he could answer, but a voice from behind us beat him to it: "'La cucaracha,' Bebita. Of course!"

Margarita glided out of the Hole and the air in the room sweetened. For just a moment the scent of fresh lilies overpowered the burnt French fry fumes that usually flavored the breeze in this Podunk town. As Glenn's mom drifted across the room, her Barbie-pink sandals clip-clopped their own little tune. A smile crossed her face when she noticed this; then she tossed her hands into the air and swiveled her size-two hips. She clapped and twirled and clip-clopped with gusto.

"*¡Ay-ay-ay! ¡Ándale!*" She executed a rapid-fire hip-swing over to the radio and flipped the station from thrash rock to her *Latina musica* station. "Come on, *Bebita. ¡Baila conmigo!*"

Her fuchsia-nailed hand grabbed my wrist and yanked me up like a rag doll. Wow, no wonder Glenn called her the Incredible Little Hulk. I made a mental note to buff up.

Glenn scrambled to his feet with all the grace of a three-legged cow in a tutu and made a beeline to the opposite side of the room. He loved Margarita to death, but there was no way he'd *baila conmigo* for her.

I had no problem with it, though. *¡Ándale!* With my barely laced work boots supplying base percussion, we made a clomp-stomp clip-clop duet. We twirled and whirled while Glenn leaned against the far wall, his dark lenses trained on us from a safe distance. Vintage Glenn: If the action steps up a notch, he steps out. And he'd been doing a lot of stepping out lately.

After a few minutes I heard Glenn's bellow over the music and our *ay-ay-ay*s. "Hey, twinkle toes! I thought you wanted to hit Binny's! Won't be open much longer!

11

We have to go now if you want to see his new stuff today!"

Binny's! All that twirling must have frappéd my brain. I'd forgotten all about the shipment.

❖ ❖ ❖

I loved the smell of Binny's. Incense smoke wafted through every nook and cranny of the shop. Chestnut. Pine. Vanilla. A smorgasbord of smells.

Then there was the eye candy. Floor to ceiling, without a break, strips of color and blocks of type assaulted my retinas.

HANG UP AND DRIVE!

MY OTHER CAR IS A TONKA.

FORGET MILK! GOT CHOCOLATE?

Bumper stickers covered every surface.

Right in the middle of it all, down at ground level on a fringed purple pillow, sat Binny. He was posed as usual— legs crossed, kneecaps jutting, gaze focused on another realm. The bell above the door had tinkled when Glenn and I strolled in, but Binny's body hadn't twitched a muscle. He was a rock.

Eventually, though, even a rock had to say hi.

"Hey there, Bluebell," he finally rasped in his swampy Big Easy accent. He pointed a crooked finger at my blue head. "My favorite color. K-pas-o, Chico Boy?"

I interrupted before Glenn could answer. "Enough chitchat. Did it come?"

Binny chuckled. He knew I'd been waiting for this shipment: a whole line of bumper stickers based entirely on cheesy quotes from even cheesier eighties movies.

"Sure I can't interest you in Shakespeare bumps, instead? *We are such stuff as dreams are made of. . . . Be not afraid of greatness. . . .*" His scratchy voice dropped lower. "Words of wisdom are food for the soul, Bluebell."

"Nope." Been there, done that. "My soul is stuffed, thank you." I already had stickers that made me think, tons and tons of them. And I had most of them committed to memory. What I wanted now was something to make me smile, to get my mind off serious stuff . . . off the eleventh. "You know what I want, Binny. Cough it up."

I jammed my fists on my hips.

"It's your soul." He shook his head and set about unwinding his pretzeled body. Grunting, he pushed himself up, then futzed a moment, trying to balance his potato-shaped torso over his chicken legs. The poor guy looked like he was trying to hula an invisible hoop. If I offered him a hand, though, he'd just smack it away and give me a look like that old lady in the market. Been there, done that, too.

Once his teetering was finally tottered out, Binny shuffled over to a row of boxes covered with a tarp. Distracted by the color-splashed walls and ceiling, I hadn't noticed the pile. With Glenn's help, Binny yanked the tarp back. "Ta-da!"—three huge boxes of bumper stickers.

"My man, Binny!" I crossed the room quickly.

Glenn sliced open the mother lode, then scooted back so I could dig in. He didn't have much use for bumper stickers unless they had cartoon characters or car logos on them. He was into graphics, just like his dad.

WHAT'S HAPPENING, HOT STUFF?!

Yeah, baby, I thought.

I FEEL THE NEED, THE NEED FOR SPEED!

That's it.

I'LL BE BACK.

Exactly what I needed. Not a serious sentiment in the bunch.

"Binmeister, you came through again. Oh hey, Glenn, here's one for you." I held up a sticker: I'D RATHER KISS A WOOKIEE.

He fake laughed and flipped me off. Then he nudged his hat to the back of his head and plunked down to the floor like a lazy dog.

Glenn may have had his dad's unruly blond hair and football bulk, but his delicate, tan face was all Margarita. The combo made for one quirky-looking pup—a mix of big and little, white and brown, rough and wimpy. He was probably trying to cancel out Margarita's sissiness with all his punky skater T-shirts and that obnoxious wallet chain he looped from his belt to the back pocket of his knee-length shorts. Not that he'd ever admit that. But the reality is, Glenn was no skater. He couldn't ride a skateboard if his life depended on it. And I was witness to the fact that his life *was* in jeopardy if he climbed on a deck: The first time

14

he'd mounted a board, he'd landed his arm in a cast. The second time, he'd landed his whole big body in traction. As far as I could see, a third time would probably be fatal.

Me, on the other hand, I could have been born on a skateboard. The deck and I were one and the same. I didn't bother with the skater rags, though. Too "type." I had my own style. It just included a board, that's all. In that way I was the reverse of Glenn—skateboarding would not lead to my immediate death. Heck, I could pick up any sport without even trying, no problem. That is, if I was interested. Which most of the time I wasn't—sweating was not my thing, either. Not too "type," just too gross.

No, it was the rest of life that threatened to put me in traction.

We hung out at Binny's shop for a while, me flipping through the stickers, Binny perched on his pillow, and Glenn sprawled on the floor by the wall. My big buddy was pretty quiet over there. In fact, he hadn't said more than a word or two since we left Dante's. But Glenn could have rougher mood swings than any girl, and when he got like that, I just had to wait him out. I wasn't about to ask him what was up his butt. Talk about a crabby old lady. So I chatted back and forth with Binny. We talked about the new stickers, McDonald's latest lunch menu, the rising price of French fries, the spin of the Earth as it danced around the sun . . . everything but what I really wanted to tell him. Finally, though, I just came out with it: "The taping is tomorrow."

Binny nodded slowly. "Indeed."

"It's the eleventh."

"All day."

"I hate the eleventh."

"Eleven is an unpleasant number. It's all straight lines. The world needs curves."

Over to the side, Glenn stayed silent. His hands, however, more than made up for his still tongue as he fiddled with an ash-filled incense tray—*click, click, click* it went as his finger swirled designs into the finely powdered ashes.

"I should just tell my dad I won't do it this year. I should just tell him no."

"Yes."

"No. I can't." I knew I couldn't. It would crush my dad. "It's the one thing he's got. All year long, nothing. No job. No friends. Nothing. Only me. The poor guy just sits there on that old lumpy futon all day."

Click, click, click.

I flipped through more stickers.

Go Ahead, Make My Day.

I GAVE HER MY HEART, SHE GAVE ME A PEN.

"You know," I went on, "he'll actually go outside after the story airs. He always does then. And people will come up to him on the street—for weeks."

Click, click, click.

Despite the fact that my dad avoided me—and life, really—I still loved him. Deep inside, he was a sweet guy. I just had to dig a little to expose the sweetness. Dig a lot, actually. In fact, archaeological excavations rarely go deeper. But I saw his soft side, occasionally, now and then. And I got an extra big peek at it once a year, right after the eleventh.

Click, click, click.

"It's almost funny," I said. "He poses and grins and waves like he knows everybody. And he always lands a few jobs after the story: welding broken gates, fixing old box springs, stuff like that. None of it requires any creativity, but they're jobs. Course, he doesn't finish any of them. But he's better to be around when he's working. Happy, even." The problem was, it all wore off after a month or two. No jobs. No happy. Just me getting stared at. "No. I can't. He needs this."

Click, click, click.

"Far be it from me to get between a girl and her daddy, Buttercup. Alls I know is, one man's happy oughtn't smother another's. Your daddy could tape that interview without you."

"Not really. Thing is—" *Click, click, click.* "Glenn, stop!"

Silence.

I took a deep breath and tried again. "Thing is, the news guys won't do the segment if I'm not part of it. And they don't want Glenn."

Glenn snorted when I said that.

Like a sniper, Binny zeroed in on him. "Don't want you, eh, Taco?"

Uh-oh. It mystified me why, but sometimes Binny got snarky with Glenn. The old man knew full well that "Taco" would rile him, every time. If I had to guess, I'd say Binny enjoyed pushing Glenn's buttons, testing how far he could go. Then again, maybe Binny just egged Glenn on in retaliation for all his snorting and clicking and gum-popping. . . .

"Ah, shoot, Binny." Glenn flung the incense holder aside. "What's up with this sissy stink, anyway? If you want to burn something, burn it. All this frou-frou smoke is lame. It's not natural."

"And just what do you call natural, oh sensitive one?" Binny challenged.

"*Smoke,* for God's sake. Real, honest-to-God smoke. Campfires. Matches. Fires. Not this jasmine crap."

"Thirty-five years of the real stuff is plenty enough. Thirty-five years of—oh, bah!" Clearly Binny didn't want to go there. He extracted a fresh incense rod from the toy quiver strapped to his back. Then he lit the tip of the scented arrow and poked it into the holder Glenn had tossed aside. Gingerly, lovingly, he set the holder on the floor next to his pillow. New smoky tendrils danced a lively tango to my nose.

Yum, lilac.

It was easy to forget Binny's past life as a firefighter. He didn't look like someone who'd once wielded heavy fire hoses like mere noodles and monkeyed up ladders into blazing infernos. He'd shriveled up since his retirement. I had this odd fear that one day he'd just blow away on the wind. A little wisp would come along, too weak to rustle a single blue hair on my own head, but it would lift him up and float him away like a flake of ash.

It had been ten years since his last fire, and he rarely talked about it, but that blaze had been a blowtorch for me and him, fusing us like pieces of welded steel. Glenn was part of that precious bond, too. But while Binny doted over me, he seemed annoyed by his connection to Glenn.

This time Glenn surprised me by hunkering into a deeper silence after Binny's jibe.

Satisfied with his target shooting for now, Binny turned his attention back to me and said, "The good Lord gave us hearts and brains, Bluebell, but it's up to us here mortals to balance the two. Your sweet ticker's right where it needs to be. It's just fielding more than its share, that's all. Time'll come for you to stand up for yourself. And when it does, you just step on up and take care of business."

Then he bowed deeply and extended his hands, palms up. Lying across them like an offering to an empress was a neon yellow bumper sticker with bold, maroon type.

My heart smiled, then my face did. I lifted my left foot and peeled off the sticker I'd wrapped around the top of my boot that morning: **If you can read this, you're too close.** Then I smoothed Binny's new one in its place: **WELL-BEHAVED WOMEN SELDOM MAKE HISTORY.** Laurel

Thatcher Ulrich, of course, from last year's prize-winning "Quotes for Cool Chicks" line.

If I had a granddaddy, I'd want him to be just like Binny.

With sudden resolve, I straightened first my droopy cutoffs and then my spineless back. "All right, then. Time to head home. Gotta get my beauty sleep for tomorrow. One way or another, it'll be a big day."

Only, I didn't know which way it would go. Around my dad, I never seemed to act the way I wanted to. And I hated being put on the spot. What did people expect me to say when they did that? "Yes, I am that total idiot loser you were thinking of, thanks for asking"?

Glenn escorted me home. His thudding footsteps alongside my skateboard made me think of my earlier goofing with Margarita. *¡Ay-ay-ay!* Silly, yes, but fun, too. I wasn't afraid to let my hair down with my friends. With them, I felt at ease. It was the rest of Earth's population that made me want to duck and cover.

If my dad had his way, though, after tomorrow I'd be front and center—again.

"Wait a sec, Glenn. Let me go in here a minute." I pointed to the ninety-nine-cent store. I'd decided to buy some purple hair dye. After tomorrow, I'd need something stronger than blue to foil the nosey-bodies. It was time to think *disguise,* not *distract.*

2

Tendrils dance around me, encircling my head like a crown. Yum, lilac. . . . Now pine. . . . Now hickory. . . . Now—what? I don't know that scent. Wait, I do know it—

Burnt rubber.

Smoldering fabric.

Charred metal.

The tendrils turn into waves, turn into blankets. Smoke is everywhere—black, heavy, choking smoke—it's in my nose—my mouth—my eyes! I can't see! Daddy, Daddy! Where are you, Daddy? I can't see you! Daddy—!

I erupted from the nightmare, heart throbbing, skin

sizzling. I lurched at my nightstand, fumbled for the switch. . . . Explosion of light! I ducked away from the lamp instinctively, but my eyes scanned the room all the same. No smoke. Just bumper stickers—walls and ceiling plastered with bumper stickers. No smoke.

No smoke.

This nightmare was worse than the others. More intense. More real. More terrifying. I buried my face in my pillow and sobbed till my shoulders ached.

My pillow smelled like burnt rubber.

3

Saturday morning, July eleventh. I kneeled on the living room futon's highest lump and peered through the dusty blinds. It looked like any other day, sunny and hot as Satan's kitchen—the usual temperature in Muessa Junction.

For a decade now, a heat wave that defied weathermen and the *Farmers' Almanac* alike had draped itself over this greasy town like a flannel blanket. Summer, fall, winter, and spring—it trapped in the French fry fumes year-round. We Junctioners barely registered the swelter anymore. Our heat-adapted bodies considered it a waste of time to leak sweat except during the most extreme of exertions.

Through the grungy screen I could see the WOPR Local 10 News van pulling into my driveway.

Let the show begin.

My dad was banging around upstairs, opening and closing and opening and closing his closet. He owned just one button-up shirt and one ratty red T-shirt, so what he expected to find each time was beyond me.

The doorbell rang, but I just plunked my rear onto the futon my dad had designed and welded years ago. No need to get the door. He was already rushing down the stairs in his blue-and-orange plaid button-up.

"I'll get it! I'll get it!" he hollered, then tripped on his shoelace. He didn't actually do a face-plant, but stumbling around with his arms flailing was more physical activity than I'd seen from him in months. When he landed against the door, he paused and took a deep breath. Not a hair on his head had moved for all the goop slathered on it, and when he casually opened the door for the news crew, he acted like Mr. Cool without looking like Mr. Fool—to them, at least. It was hard to believe this man was once internationally respected for his innovative futon designs.

"Come in, come in." He welcomed them into his palace with a regal arm-swoop. Not that there was anything kingly about my dad. Short and slight like me, he wore the Kent family button eyes on a head too square for hats, and his sad-sack cheeks and droopy shoulders exuded about as much charm as a hunk of moldy cheese.

Our guests poured into the stale, dark room like

champagne into a trucker's boot. I recognized the feature reporter. She was new to the station and new to Muessa Junction, but everyone knew who she was because her big smile and bigger boobs had raised the newscast's ratings sky-high.

"Selina Nashashibi, WOPR Local Ten News." She said it like she was beginning a broadcast, not like she was stepping into a run-down tract home. Sweat glistened above her flawlessly painted lips, proof that she was an outsider. Her eyes cased the room as she spoke.

"Welcome, Ms. Nasha . . . shasha . . . shasabi," bumbled my dad. "Pick it up, there, George. Ha-ha."

George was the cameraman who filmed the segment every year. I liked him, a go-with-the-flow kind of guy who treated me like any other annoying teenager.

Selina took charge. "Mr. Kent, everything I've heard about you makes me proud to stand here today. This humble community would be very different if it weren't for you. You put a sleepy little blue-collar town on the map as a landmark of higher education. I—" She noticed me on the futon.

Here we go.

"Oh, could this be Monalisa Kent?" she asked.

"Could be," I replied.

"Yes, ma'am! This is my daughter, Mona." My dad rushed over and tried to get me to stand up and shake Selina's hand.

Might as well get it over with. I stood up and curtsied,

my hand outstretched. Our skin barely touched as we shook hands. Selina looked me up and down, taking in my blue hair, my logo-spattered cycling top, my patent-leather mini, and my spit-shined dress-up biker boots. She paused extra long on the fresh bumper sticker I'd wrapped around my left boot: I GOT OUT OF BED FOR *THIS*?

What, do I clash?

"Remind me how old you are, Mona."

Remind you? I haven't told you, lady. "Sixteen."

Her bright lips moved slightly as she counted backward. "Oh, that's right. Ten years ago you'd just turned six. Awfully young to be playing with fire."

She pivoted on her spiked heel and started ordering George around, telling him where she wanted the lights and how she wanted him to film her. He just set up the way he did every year: my dad in the middle of the futon, me next to him, and room for the reporter on the far side. Selina didn't look so thrilled about resting her delicate derriere there, but the only other furniture was a couple of splintered bar stools over by the kitchen bar.

Helping George with all the cables and lights—none of the other reporters used so many lights!—was a spindly little kid, maybe twelve or thirteen, with hair that was way too black to be natural. Kind of Goth. Kind of cool.

George caught me checking out his lackey. "This is my nephew Burt. He's helping me out this summer. Say hey to Mona, Burt."

The kid scurried over and stuck out a scrawny hand. "Hey!"

I hesitated, then put my hand in his. He pumped it briskly. "Hey to you," I said.

The kid grinned and scurried back to adjust a light, his movements herky-jerky. I saw George cringe at the fidgety manhandling of his precious equipment, but he didn't say a word.

"Ready, everyone, ready." Selina was ready, so everyone was ready. She nodded at George, who shouldered his camera and counted down with his fingers: 3, 2, 1—

"This is Selina Nashashibi, reporting to you from the home of local hero Mac Kent. It was ten years ago today that the world-renowned Wayne Furniture Plant went up in flames, nearly taking this entire town with it. Our award-winning, exclusive WOPR Local Ten News archived footage captured the raging inferno." Here they would edit in George's images from that night. After nine of these tapings, I had the sequence memorized. "July eleventh— the day Mackenzie Kent went from mild-mannered futon frame manager to lifesaving, town-saving superhero. Mac"—here George would zoom out from Selina's face to fit my dad into the frame—"you saved the lives of two children that night, five-year-old Paco Glenn and your own six-year-old daughter, Monalisa. Would you tell me, in your own words"—*duh*—"what you and the kids were doing at the plant that evening?"

"I'd be happy to, Ms. Nasha . . . wasa . . . sasa . . . er, ma'am." My dad scrunched up his face like he was trying hard to remember. I'd caught him practicing that expression in the window of the microwave that morning. "See, Wayne Furniture was a family-owned plant. Just about everybody in town worked there. And, well, old Mr. W. and me had an agreement, an understanding, if you will. I was the futon frame manager, and if I thought my being at the plant after hours was necessary to secure the futon work floor for safety reasons, I should be there, no question. Safety first. And being a single parent and all, I had to bring Mona with me sometimes. Mr. W. was okay with that. He understood, being a family man himself. That night I was looking after Mona's little friend, too."

Selina was staring intently at him, nodding her head like there was nothing on the planet more riveting than the words tripping off SuperMac's tongue. Burt was perched on the edge of a bar stool behind his uncle, just as fascinated. Me, I just sat there like a statue. My jaw ached from clenching my teeth.

My dad went on. "My little Mona"—here it came, George zooming back to fit me in the frame, my dad lifting his hand to ruffle my hair—"she was just a tyke. Curious, that's all. She didn't mean no harm." *Ruffle, ruffle.*

Burt was grinning now.

Little punk.

Selina jumped in. "Let's talk about that a moment, Mac. I'm told that Mona set the fire."

Burt's grin vanished.

"Well, yes, ma'am. Unfortunately that's the way of it. Mona don't remember none of it, but the fire chief pieced together what happened. He figures Mona saw me testing a blowtorch. See, it was safety protocol for me to turn the equipment on and off now and then, make sure stuff was in working order. I feel real bad that I turned my back on the kids, 'cause like I said, Mona's curious—just like her dear momma. . . ." His breath caught, the mere mention of my mom instantly knocking him to the edge of another "I miss your dear momma" funk. But he pulled himself out of the nosedive. "I thought Mona knew not to touch things in the plant; she never did nothing like that before. She was a good kid. Really. Still is."

There! Good thing I didn't sneeze or I might've missed it: My dad had his sweet side. So what if the broadcast intensified the staring for a while? I could handle it. Even Superman has his kryptonite. And really, I deserved it, didn't I? I mean, I torched a huge factory, nearly burned the entire town right off the map, and put hundreds of people out of work. I was a loser of the highest order. Considering my crime, I was getting off easy with some bitter looky-loo staring.

"Let's take another look at Local Ten's exclusive footage of the burning plant," Selina said. "Fire Chief Gordon's report states that when Mona turned on that blowtorch, the foam futon mattresses ignited immediately, and the rest of the furniture-making materials fed the fire like kindling. It's amazing any of you made it out alive. But you kept your wits about you, Mac, and you got the kids out. Slow-motion footage shows you emerging from a wall of flame, a child under each arm, flames catching on your shirt. Mac, you're a hero."

"I did what I had to, Selina." My dad turned and gazed right at me. His eyes were moist. His lower lip trembled.

I hadn't seen him practice that.

"Nothing mattered at that moment but getting Paco and Mona out. I didn't even know I was on fire. The firemen blasted me with hoses, and when I fell, they ran up and grabbed the kids and then sprayed me with fire extinguishers and . . . well, then . . . then . . ."

I was getting that Twinkie feeling again.

Selina jumped into my dad's emotional pause. "That's when photographer Farley McKnabb snapped his Pulitzer Prize–winning photo of Mona and firefighter Binford Petit. That photo ran on the cover of every major newspaper and magazine in the country." Next they would cut to the photo that appeared on *Time* and *Rolling Stone* and *Newsweek.* . . . I didn't need to see the image again; I had it memorized, wide blue eyes and all. "That coverage garnered national attention for the small-town fire, and when the Wayne family decided not to reopen the plant and left nearly five hundred people out of work, you stepped up to the plate once again, Mac. You spoke to the country, and the country listened. Will you repeat your famous words for me?"

My dad puffed his chest out and pointed his chin right at the camera, his tears suddenly dried up. "I said, 'We got a big ol' school up the street, what do we need a stupid furniture plant for anyways?'"

"That humble statement," Selina said, "rallied the townspeople around its remaining asset and turned this dying blue-collar town into a cause célèbre for the entire country. Muessa Junction arose from the ashes to become a mecca for higher education, home to an institution that draws the brightest of America's youth. Professors and valedictorians from every corner of the United States now call Muessa Junction University home. Today, just ten years after that fateful night, MJU employs more townspeople than the Wayne plant ever did. And the supporting shops and fast-food restaurants employ just about everyone else. You, Mr. Kent, are a national hero."

And you, Monalisa Kent, are a national loser.

Burt's mouth hung open. I guess he hadn't realized he was in the same room as the biggest loser to walk the planet—the girl who torched the town. Lucky for him, WOPR Local 10 News believes in rubbing people's faces in their own screwups once a year. Now he knew That Monalisa Kent Girl when he saw her. And to think they'd almost let someone slip into town who hadn't been alerted to hate my guts. *Thank goodness we dodged that bullet, Tonto.*

I'd reached my limit. Selina became just a set of flapping lips to me as she wound down the interview, and my dad was nothing more than a bobbing head. As soon as I could, I skulked off to my room and shut the door.

I lay on my bed like a corpse. My face was roasting and my stomach was woozy.

Selena is an idiot. She didn't even bother to ask me anything. Not that I would've bothered to answer her. . . .

Holding my breath calmed the woozing, so I sucked in big gulps of air, then held them as long as I could. Being in my room helped, too. All around me, bumper stickers covered every surface—my walls, my door, my ceiling, my bedposts and headboard, my desk and dresser and closet, and, as of last week, half of my floor. Some people might have found it dizzying, but to me it was like climbing into a cozy, bullet-proof safe. I counted silently and read my ceiling for strength.

DON'T BELIEVE EVERYTHING YOU THINK.

Knock, knock.

Exhale. "Go away." Deep breath.

AUNTIE EM: HATE YOU, HATE KANSAS, TAKING THE DOG.— DOROTHY.

"Can I come in?"

I didn't recognize the voice.

"It's Burt. Can I come in?"

Burt? Exhale. "Uh . . . yeah, I guess."

I sat up and hung my legs over the side of my bed. Burt poked his jet-black head around the door, then slipped the rest of his body through the opening. Good thing he was so skinny.

"Hey," he said.

The kid had quite a vocabulary. "Hey."

"Jeez. Guess you like bumper stickers."

"Guess so."

"Got a car to put 'em on?"

It was on the tip of my tongue to tell the shrimp to scram. Yet seeing him standing there, his hands in his back pockets and his neck contorting like Gumby to examine my stickered sanctuary, something stopped me. I followed his line of vision with my eyes and saw that he was reading the sticker above my pillow: **THE BIGGEST DRAGON IS THE ONE IN THE MIRROR.**

"No," I answered. "No car. I've got my own parking spot reserved at school already. Car's next."

"I'm getting a car the minute I get my license."

"Is that so?"

"Yep. Just two years, twenty-seven days, eight hours, and"—he consulted his watch—"thirty-three minutes to go. Which means I get my permit in *one* year, twenty-seven days, eight hours, and—"

"Thirty-three minutes."

"That's right!"

"What do you know."

An awkward silence settled in as he stood there by the door, hands still in his pockets, rocking heel-toe, his eyes roaming the room.

I started swinging my legs.

Burt contorted his neck again to see the stickers above the door behind him. Still he said nothing.

I started looking around, too.

BEAM ME UP, SCOTTY.

The silence continued.

I DON'T WANT THE WHOLE WORLD, I JUST WANT YOUR HALF.

Silence could be awfully loud.

VERY FUNNY, SCOTTY. NOW BEAM DOWN MY CLOTHES!

I was starting to clue in that this wasn't awkward for Burt at all. Well, heck, maybe that was because *he* hadn't just had to sit there in some supposed "interview" as the token symbol of Loserdom for all the world to see—*again*. What was some puny, punky Goth doing in my room, anyway? This was my space, these were my words on the wall. . . . *He* should have been the one feeling awkward, not *me*.

"So, Burt—what do you want?"

He stopped rocking. "Did you really torch the place?"

And there you have it, Sherlock. The boy wanted the skinny, the lowdown, straight from the horse's mouth. Gotta give credit where credit was due, though: Not many people had the chutzpah to come right out and ask me. Staring at me with total loathing on their faces was easier. "So they tell me. I don't remember."

"Like amnesia?"

"Something like that."

34

"Maybe you just don't want to remember. Maybe that's what's wrong with you."

"Are you kidding me?" I was on my feet so quickly I stumbled on the bedspread. No arm-flailing, though. "You barge into a girl's bedroom and tell her what's wrong with her? Does that usually work for you, Burt?"

He whipped his arms up as if to ward off attack. "Hey, whoa . . ."

No *whoa*. I wasn't done yet. The kid had hit a sensitive nerve, the one that flared up whenever I tried to figure out why my stupid brain denied me access to my own memories. That nerve felt especially raw lately as more and more snippets of memory broke free and scared the bejesus out of me. Nightmares . . . creepy visions . . . sudden flashbacks. Just about anything set them off. And each one was worse than the one before it. More detailed. More painful.

"You don't know anything about this, Burt. You don't know anything about me."

"I'm sorry. Really." His face was all scrunched up, like he was confused. "You didn't say anything back there, that's all. Why didn't you say anything? I'll bet you're hiding a plethora of emotion."

A "plethora"? What happened to "hey"?

I bit back my next harsh words. The kid sounded sincere—like he cared, even—so I dialed my trigger-happy temper down a notch. I could do a notch. After all, Burt's confusion was only fair. It matched my own. Why *couldn't* I remember? I didn't know. And if I couldn't remember what I did, how would I ever be able to defend myself? I didn't know that, either. What I did know was that Junctioners blamed me for turning them into flunkies kowtowing to spoiled rich kids. Who could blame them for being ticked off about that?

"Look, Burt. I just want to get through a day—one single day—without everyone judging me. That's all." I pitched my voice deeper. "'There's That Monalisa Kent Girl, the fire starter.' It gets old, you know, being the bad guy."

"But Selina said you were only six."

"People don't care. Not when you're famous, they don't—especially when you're famous for something bad. When everyone knows who you are, they think they know who you are, you know? I'm That Monalisa Kent Girl. I'm not a real person."

He looked like he was thinking about that a moment. "Yeah, I guess that would be hard." He turned to the wall at his left and slid his fingers along a pale blue sticker showing a white hand shaking a black hand, from the "Yin Meets Yang" line. "I'd probably hide in my room, too."

"I'm not *hiding* in my room." *Deep breath, Mona, deep breath*. I focused on my glorious, sloganed walls. **ON THE OTHER HAND, YOU HAVE DIFFERENT FINGERS.** "This is my space. In here, I hear stuff I want to hear. Stuff that makes me happy, makes me laugh. I surround myself with words and thoughts that express me—the *real* me."

"You wrote these?"

"Course not." Just when I thought he might be showing signs of intelligent life—a rare thing in Muessa Junction. "I handpicked every one of them, though. They're definitely me."

Burt didn't look convinced. He didn't need to be. Only Binny truly got it. Glenn *thought* he got it, but he didn't, not really. Which was okay. I loved Glenn anyway. He was like a big brother who happened to be younger than me. He watched over me, made me feel safe.

Glenn did get that I refused to hide in my house and let life pass me by like my dad did. But it was frazzling to be out and about and have people staring at you like you just kicked their cat. Aren't crowds supposed to make you anonymous?

A sticker over Burt's shoulder caught my eye: I FEEL LIKE I'M DIAGONALLY PARKED IN A PARALLEL UNIVERSE. *Amen.*

My Twinkie tummy was settling down.

Burt was scratching his ear and nibbling his lip, working hard to understand. My dad's face had squinched in all the same places when he saw my blue hair yesterday. Frankly it blew my mind that he'd even registered the color change, having been in an especially deep "I miss your dear momma" fest for days. Then he went and really knocked me for a loop by mumbling, "Pretty color, sweetie," and forcing up a weak smile. My dad had his moments. I took them as they came.

"Well, I don't want to be fake, either," Burt finally

declared. Then he took a deep, cleansing breath and patted his rumbling tummy. His puppy-dog grin snapped back into place. "I'm hungry. Wanna get something to eat? I'm done with Uncle George for the day. He lets me do whatever while he edits the show. Really, he's just worried I'll mess up his editing room—just because one time I pressed some buttons. He'd already pressed the same buttons, so I don't know what the big deal was. Anyway, I'm starving. Let's get a hamburger. My treat."

"Your treat?"

"Yeah. My mom is a psychologist."

My own squinchy face must have tipped him off that further information was required.

"People pay her lots of money to sit there," he explained, "while they talk about other people and all the stuff that gets done to them. Then she tells them if they don't like it, do something about it. Seems like a racket to me, but I get a pretty cool allowance out of it. So do you want to?"

Aw, heck, why not let the little guy buy me lunch? It beat lying around thinking about my dad and Twinkies. **CARPE DIEM**. I agreed to the date, but only if Glenn could come along.

"Friend, or boyfriend?" Burt asked.

"Does it matter?"

He shrugged. "I guess not. Just checking the lay of the land, that's all."

Yep, the kid had chutzpah.

Since neither of us owned a car, Burt and I had to hoof it to the Pink Cloud—me on my board, of course. We didn't have far to go, actually. University or no, Muessa Junction wasn't big, and my house was barely a mile from the center of it. Along the way, clumps of tall buildings poked from the ground like soggy fries in a supersize box. Lapped by hazy waves of heat, the buildings always looked wilted and sad.

Burt skipped ahead, making a game of kicking the crusty burger wrappers and greasy, balled-up paper bags that littered the sidewalk. He skipped blindly past the man in the red and yellow overalls without even noticing him. I didn't miss the guy, though. He was lounging on the curb in the shade of a parked Wienerschnitzel delivery truck, leaning against the front passenger tire with a tall white soda cup in his hand and a hot dog balanced precariously on his bent knees. He lazily watched Burt dribble-kick a crumpled bag past. Then he spotted me. His face scrunched up in puzzlement, then slid into ugliness.

He flung a leg straight out across the sidewalk, blocking my path. His hot dog fell into the gutter as I skidded to a stop.

"I know you," he said. "You're That Monalisa Kent Girl, aren't you?"

"No," I said, stomping on the back of my skateboard, popping it up into my hand.

"I think you are." He left his leg in my path. "I got a bone to pick with you."

My stomach fluttered. It had been years since anyone openly confronted me like this. Usually after they asked me if I was *her,* I just denied my existence and made a quick getaway. Junctioners tend to believe whatever you tell them, at least for a few minutes. Then they make up their mind and that is that, forever and ever, amen.

"I'm not who you're talking about," I said, averting eye contact so he wouldn't think I was challenging him. I wondered what would happen if I tried to step over his leg. "Can I get by, please?"

His leg stayed put.

Up ahead, Burt whooped in excitement and darted up the twisted old climbing tree in front of Burger King.

I eyed the guy on the ground. He had a potbelly, and his face was jowly. There was no way he could scramble up and catch me if I only managed to get past him. Maybe if I had a distraction . . .

"Look at this truck." He pounded his elbow backward into the tire. "You think I like driving this beast all day? I don't. I hate it. I'm an upholsterer, and a damn good one, not some flunky driver."

I looked forward for Burt again. He was hanging upside down from a branch, his knees folded over the top, the back of his head facing us. I'd get no help there.

"You know why I'm driving this truck? Do you?"

I didn't answer. He didn't really want an answer, I

learned that a long time ago. No one wanted to hear from me, they just wanted me to stand there while they heaped more guilt on my already sagging shoulders. I had enough of that, thank you. What I needed was to get away. Slowly I raised my skateboard up a few inches.

"You. You're the reason I'm driving this godforsaken truck. What do you think of that, girly? What do you think of the pathetic shell of a man you've turned me into?"

THIS is what I think of it! I shoved the skateboard down on the man's shin as hard as I could. He screamed and pulled his leg to his chest, dropping his soda to clutch his shin. I bolted away, throwing my board to the ground in front of me, and then jumped on and push, push, pushed with my right leg as fast as I could.

"C'mon, Burt!" I yelled as I flew past the tree. "Hurry up!"

Burt dropped to the root-cracked dirt like a cat and raced after me. "What? What's the rush?"

"Just come on." I glanced quickly over my shoulder. The guy was balled up next to the tire, rocking and clutching his leg. He wasn't going anywhere soon.

I slowed down. I'd made a clean getaway. This time.

I couldn't remember the last time someone had gotten in my face that bad. Maybe after ten years this town had finally reached its limit. I know I had. I was sick of being their fall guy. I only wished I would've said something to that jerk before I bolted, something clever and witty to make him feel stupid for treating me like some piece of trash. If I were as smart as those people who wrote the bumper stickers wallpapering my bedroom, then this town would've been sorry. But I wasn't that smart. I was just That Monalisa Kent Girl, the fire starter. Accident or not, it *was* my fault this guy was schlepping for some mind-numbing fast-food company instead of creating furniture for kings, and there was nothing I could say or do to fix that now. And when someone had a problem with that, I just had to skulk away before things turned from bad to worse.

I let Burt catch up to me. He started jabbering about tree sitters and how cool it would be to live in a tree for a few weeks or months at a time. It distracted me from dwelling on what I'd just done. I'd never hit anyone before, but the guy left me no other way out. And I had to admit, it felt kind of good to make him move. Satisfying.

When Burt and I finally reached the Pink Cloud, we stopped below the fluffy, cloud-shaped awning over Margarita's golden-gated glass door. Burt's eyes widened and he grinned broadly.

"It's like crossing into heaven," he said reverently as he pushed open the heavy door and got his first look at the place I considered my second home—the first being Dante's.

Inside, the large rosy room was immaculate, showing no signs of Friday night's bustle. The pink blinds on the immense shopwindow were raised high, letting the morning sun slide across the glossy checkered floor and bounce off the metal frames of four frilly pink tattoo chairs along the far wall. Glinting silver tracks lined the ceiling above each chair, dangling velvety rose drapes that could be tugged around for privacy. Silver-framed car posters dotted the walls. Steps from the door, a glass display case filled with belly rings, nose studs, and other jewelry supported a large cash register and a sign propped on a tiny easel: No One Under 18 Beyond This Point. To the right of the display case, a pink suede futon faced three pink beanbag chairs, all sprinkled on a white shag throw rug. A glass coffee table separated the futon and beanbags, with magazines fanned atop it in a soft arc. An espresso machine hummed softly in the corner next to an ultrasonic sterilizer. The air smelled of coffee and roses.

The Pink Cloud was definitely a lot of pink to swallow, but cutting through it was better than entering the Glenns' realm through the Dante's door. If I went in through Tuck's entrance, I'd have to endure the sight of the burnt-out plant across the street from his shop. University recruiting pamphlets described my town as circular, like a wagon wheel, with the plant as its hub. But I didn't see it that way. In my mind, Muessa Junction was more like a large campfire ring with the plant at its center—a glowing ember surrounded by miles of coal-black streets and ashy buildings. The roads and shops closest to the plant were always the hottest.

That the plant's charred corpse still stood after all

these years amazed me. But the Cranky Society of Old People or something like that wanted to preserve the structure as a historical monument, like a pathetic memorial to the town's pre-Whopperization, so they kept stopping the bulldozers.

And preserving my pain.

I was happy inside Dante's, though, with its thick walls between me and the plant. The key was to move to and through the Hole quickly—no lingering in the Pink Cloud. Margarita could be kind of creepy sometimes, and being in the shop with her one-on-one for too long was risky. Sooner or later, she'd start pumping me about boys or my dreams or other random stuff. Margarita fancied herself the mother I never had—and never needed, if you ask me. True, on the day I was born my mom died, and yes, sometimes I wondered what it would be like to have a mom around, but mostly I felt okay about it, since I never knew what it was like to have a mom around in the first place. I tried not to be rude to Margarita about it, though. With all the stories she had about growing up with her own beloved *Mamita*—a cook/philosopher who was practically worshiped back in Mexico City—it wasn't any wonder that my attitude seemed as wrong to her as refried beans on Wonder Bread.

It took some nudging and pulling, but I was able to hustle Burt around the bejeweled display case, past the multi-angle tattoo chairs, and into the Hole. You'd think he never saw a tattoo chair before—he actually started climbing on one and I had to yank the hyper little monkey by his back belt loops to wrench him free of it. Then he made a move toward the open closet door, where someone was rummaging—probably Talula, who was in charge of Margarita's supplies. I held on to his pants firmly and dragged him into the Hole. When we emerged on the Dante's side, we found Glenn in his usual spot—lounging on the dark blue futon under the air conditioner vent, his eyes staring up dreamily at the ceiling mural of King Arthur's dragon-besieged castle. Actually I was almost surprised to find him in the usual spot. Several times last week I'd shown up and he was AWOL.

I smacked Glenn's foot to get his attention. He immediately aimed his dark lenses at Burt. "Who's this?"

"This is Burt. Say hey, Burt."

"Hey!" The kid stuck out his hand.

Glenn didn't do anything for a moment. Then he hauled himself to his feet, slowly. I almost laughed as Burt's eyes followed my big buddy up, up, up. "I didn't know they were giving away puppies at the supermarket again," Glenn said.

"Heel, Fido. Burt's treating me to a burger. I told him you have to come, though. I need a chaperone. This guy's almost old enough to drive. I need someone to keep an eye on him, make sure he doesn't get fresh over fries. You up for it?"

"Burgers?" The magic word. "Sure, I'm game."

Even with dark glasses and bum eyes that got messed

up in the fire, Glenn never missed a detail. He looked down at Burt, still standing there with his scrawny hand out and his loopy grin. Then Glenn yawned and stretched high to exaggerate the height difference even more. I half expected him to lift his leg and pee on the futon to mark his territory.

Instead he slapped the kid's outstretched hand in a sideways high five. "What's shakin', Burt? I'm Glenn."

"*Paco* Glenn?" Guess Burt didn't miss much, either.

"Glenn will be fine." He lurched away and wedged himself into the Hole to fetch his sacred Batman ball cap.

I quickly whispered to Burt, "Kids used to call him *Taco* instead of *Paco.*"

"That's nothing," he whispered back. "Try being a Burt."

Burt . . . Lurt . . . Murt . . . ?

When Glenn reemerged from the Hole, Tuck was following him. How those two behemoths fit in that tiny room had to be the Ninth Wonder of the World. Tuck's arms were stacked high with pink towels that he must have swiped from Margarita's cabinets. Dante's never seemed to have enough clean towels.

"Pop," said Glenn, "this is Burt."

Tuck poked his head around the towels. "What's that? Burp?"

Oh.

"Just yankin' your chain, kid." Tuck had a booming voice, one that rumbled around in his cavernous chest, building up power before bellowing forth. His vibrating Adam's apple caught my eye. It now had a coat of arms etched over it, positioned like a tag on the dog collar that Margarita had tattooed around his neck years ago. Sometimes she joked about having studs implanted in collar-covered skin so he'd look like a big bulldog, but she hadn't done it yet. The flesh under the coat of arms was puffy and flushed. The tattoo was fresh. "Welcome to Dante's Inferno, Ink."

Burt didn't hear Tuck, though. The kid was doing his Gumby neck routine. Only this time he added audio: "Oh wow. . . . Aw, man. . . . Look at that . . . ! This is so cool . . . ! Oooh, that had to hurt. . . ." The steel-plated walls he admired were dotted with taped-up Polaroids of tattooed body parts, and two display racks full of brightly colored tattoo magazines, postcards, and design sets were bolted to the floor just inches away from him. Burt was wildy spinning one of the racks with his left hand, but he was too busy Gumbying the rest of the room to give any real attention to the spinning rack.

Tuck laughed and dropped his fluffy stack on the futon. "Like what you see, kid? Too bad your timing ain't better. A few minutes earlier and you'd of seen the work of the finest tattoo artist ever to crank up a needle."

"No!" I blurted. "The Guy was here? Just now?"

"Sure was. His canvas walked out of here not ten minutes ago. Another Dante's exclusive." Tuck was as happy as a clam—if clams could be happy. "Awesome work! I never seen anything like it. And he's so fast. A genius, pure and simple. Michelangelo with a needle." He grabbed a pink towel from the stack and a bottle of disinfectant to sterilize a tattoo chair.

"I can help!" Burt rushed toward Tuck, snatching a towel along the way and spilling the rest of the stack to the floor.

"Who'd he ink?" I pointed to the pink pile at Glenn's feet. He stooped to pick them up. "And why's it so quiet around here?"

"I chased everyone off. The Guy wants his privacy, the Guy gets his privacy." Tuck pulled the towel out of Burt's hands and playfully flicked Glenn on the rear with it as he bent over. Burt saw that and tried to flick his towel, too, narrowly missing Tuck's thigh. The kid didn't know how lucky he was. "He inked some rocker dude from up north this time," Tuck said.

"Really? Aw, Glenn, why didn't you call me?" Could this day get any worse?

"Yeah, right, that's what I should've done." He tossed the last towel onto the futon and stood tall again. "Your pop would've freaked if I'd called during the taping, and you know it. Then you'd just bust my hump for upsetting him."

"No, I wouldn't."

"Yes, you would. You *know* you would. Anyway, Pop's not kidding that the Guy won't come around here anymore if we start fielding an audience. You know

48

exactly what I'm talking about, Miss Everybody Stop Staring At Me."

I made a sputtering noise. I was done, cooked, burnt to a crisp. I'd spent my morning being raked over the coals—for the millionth time—and then got threatened in front of a wiener truck for something I could never undo. Now those oh-so-joyful experiences had made me miss out on catching a legend in action. It wasn't even noon yet; imagine what the rest of the day would bring—or the rest of my *life*, for that matter. When my dad's interview hits the airwaves, I'll have to fall back into serious duck-and-cover mode again. Being infamous really sucks the moxie out of a girl. "Just forget it. I don't care about some stupid tattoo guy anyway."

I kicked the wad of towels back onto the floor, then clomp-stomped out the Dante's door, nearly plowing Potter Pete onto his Potter butt in the doorway. A Dante's regular, Potter was bent down in the doorway, picking up a penny—

Hold the train, Clyde! "Potter, what is that on your head?"

"Like it?" He went into a formal bow, giving me a long, full-view shot of the brand-new bull's-eye tattooed smack on top of his shaved head. Who would've thought to get a tattoo there? Ow. Shades of angry pink skin ringed the image.

Being bent over like that gave Potter a good look at my boots. " 'I got up for this?' " he read out loud. Then he stood up, smiling, and pet the top of my head with a tat-tooed hand. "That's a good one, Mona. Way better than that lovey-dovey Zen junk you had the other day. Hey, Tuck, fire up that needle, will ya? I got me a bald spot on my left ankle that needs beautifying."

Caught off guard by Potter's newly targeted head, I was speechless—again. So I kept right on stomping—only, I kept a hand up to the side of my face to shield my eyes from the plant, like a blinder on a one-eyed horse. I'd been dumb enough to go out the Dante's door without think-ing; I wasn't dumb enough to let my eyes land on the plant. Not by a long shot.

Salty fries. Ketchup-slathered cheeseburger. Chilly choco-late shake to wash it all down. Just what the doctor or-dered. A meal to soothe the anguished soul.

I'd figured out a long time ago that I could drown my sorrows under the Golden Arches, and I've been hooked on fast food ever since. Red-wigged clowns inside, jungle gyms outside, apple pies for dessert . . . who could be cranky in a place where even the meals were happy?

Plus, neither I nor my dad could cook our way out of a macaroni box, so it was eat out or starve. Now and then I stocked our fridge with frozen dinners to keep my dad from wasting away, but my own meals came from the school cafeteria or McDonald's or Burger King or some such. Even though it wasn't huge, my mom's insurance settlement was enough to keep my dad's freezer full of Swedish Meatball Supreme and my gut full of cheeseburgers.

The shake snailed a frozen trail down my food pipe. *Ahhhhh.* My shoulders unclenched. I dipped a fry into my cup of frosty goo. Across the restaurant, some frizzy-bearded geezer in a plastic booth had me in his sights. I looked away quickly as I stuffed the fry into my mouth. Heaven forbid I try to eat without someone watching me. Maybe I should just be happy he didn't come over and stick his leg across my table, complaining about having a bone to pick with me.

While I chewed, I outlined to Burt and Glenn my plan to lie low for a few days. They'd caught up with me about a block from Dante's.

"The interview airs tonight," I said, "so starting Sunday everyone will have fire on the brain. I just need to keep a low profile for a while. Make my mug scarce, you know?"

It being summer, I didn't need to strategize about school—my only lucky break on a not-so-lucky day. For the most part, the other kids ignored me in the halls and classrooms anyway. And that was fine by me. I had my friends at Dante's and didn't need more. Besides, being ignored was better than being the center of unwanted attention. I hated those days when the other kids remembered I was evil incarnate. And there was always a Selina around to remind them if it slipped their minds for long. The brainless morons. Muessa Junction High was a cattle ranch—much like the rest of Muessa Junction. The student body merely headed where herded, chewing their cud, eyes glazed over. Future Pink Cloud customers. I expected to see every rotten one of them eventually flinching under Margarita's needle, branding their heinies with hearts and flowers simply because it was the Thing to Do.

Maybe I should just take off for a bigger city. Big means crowded. Crowded means anonymous. At least it's supposed to. I guess no one told old Frizzbeard that. He was still watching me across the crowd.

"You could come be a rodeo clown with me," Burt said, then slurped hard on his straw.

Glenn stopped chewing and turned his dark glasses from his drippy burger to Burt. "You're going to be a rodeo clown?"

"Maybe. If I like it. I'm going to my uncle Brody's after summer's over. It's his turn."

"His turn?"

"Yeah. All my aunts and uncles take turns with me. I get to live with each of them for a while and they teach me what they know. Mom calls it mind molding. She lectures on it. Says it's important for kids to assimilate other places and people and jobs and stuff. Mom is famous."

Now there was an intriguing theory. Your own parents pushing you to get out and see the world, to try new things, to shake things up, to assimilate. Hey, I was all for gettin' outta Dodge. "So you never see your parents?"

"Sometimes I do. They visit me and we talk on the

phone and e-mail a lot. Mom says kids are curious and need experiences to satisfy their curiosity. I have a plethora of experiences now. I don't even have to do regular school. The next place I go to is . . . uh . . ." He dug a wad of paper out of his pocket and uncrumpled it to read the scribbled address. "Fort Worth, Texas. My uncle Brody is a rodeo clown there. By the end of the summer I'll be diving into barrels and getting rolled by raging bulls. I saw a picture of Uncle Brody in a barrel once. It was ten feet off the ground!"

"Ten feet?" Glenn gaped. "That's cool."

"About as cool as standing on a train track waiting for the Little Engine That Could," I said.

"Try not to be such a girl, Mona."

"I am a girl, Einstein."

"Here, have a French fry." Burt held up a red cardboard container between us. Glenn took one. I pointed down at my own pile of fries.

Burt set down the container and used both tiny hands to pick up his hamburger again. I never guessed they made almost-fourteen-year-olds so small. "Maybe no one will see your dad's interview."

"They'll see it," Glenn mumbled, exposing a chewed fry. Gross.

"But they won't really give her a hard time, will they?"

"Yeah, they will. Mostly they'll be on her case in stores and restaurants, places where people check out other people more. They don't usually say anything, though, just stare at her like they want to kick her butt. It's all so stupid. I mean, yeah she screwed up, but it's not like she stuck up a bank or something. She was a kid. It was an accident." He jabbed his hamburger in the air at me. "You know what I think? I think people just got scared."

"Scared of Mona?" Burt asked.

Yes, I thought.

"No," Glenn said. "Scared that if the plant left, the town would die. They'd lose everything."

"And that would be Mona's fault?"

Yes.

"No. But they'd blame her anyway."

You got that right. Weinerschnitzel man was proof of that.

As I worked to extract a nasty ridged green disc—a pickle, some claimed—from the lid of my burger bun, Glenn leaned forward on both elbows and took a deep breath, the way he did whenever he tried to help me make sense of hypotenuses and isosceles and Pythagorean theorems. *Look out now, Burt.* Glenn liked it when people asked him questions. Knowing the answers probably made him feel like a big shot. And he always knew the answers. And clearly Burt was full of questions.

"Listen, Burt," said Professor Glenn. "When you get scared, you get mad. You can't help it. Think about it for a minute. Say I leaped out at you from behind a door. You'd jump, right? No way not to. Okay, yeah, you might laugh a little, but I guarantee you, at the very least you'd jump and then sock me in the arm—probably pretty hard and not really joking. That's just how it is. Being chicken makes people madder than cocks. And they'll do anything not to feel like that again."

At that, he tore open a ketchup packet with his teeth. Then he squeezed the blood-red goo directly into his mouth, turning his tongue into a horror movie cliche. He nodded thanks when I tossed my green disc onto his wrapper.

"You know," he went on, his fangs dripping red, "I bet if Mona *had* robbed a bank, she'd be a hero, like a girl Jesse James. *He's* a hero. Which is stupid."

"Yeah, stupid." Burt made a face like he just sucked something sour.

Burt watched Glenn squeeze the last drips of ketchup into his mouth a moment, then grabbed a packet of his own and copied the horror-movie maneuver. Only, his attempt spurted a glob across the table at me. "Oh, sorry, Mona." He grabbed a bunch of napkins and lunged for my chest. I blocked his lunge and snatched the napkins. There were some things a girl had to do for herself. "How come Jesse James is a hero, anyway? Didn't he kill people?"

"When you figure it out, Burto, you let me know."

Glenn tucked my disc into the remnants of his burger and chomped down with gusto. Seeing that, Burt jolted into action, tearing apart his own hamburger in search of green. He proudly plunked the supposed veggie onto Glenn's wrapper, earning his own thanks nod.

Yep, the kid was quick. He'd already figured out the way to Glenn's heart.

Across the restaurant, Frizzbeard was *still* staring at me. He was trying to figure out how he knew me. I could tell because I'd seen that puzzled, squinched-up expression a million times before—always directed at me, usually followed by "Aren't you That Monalisa Kent Girl?" Well, if he didn't put it together now, he would when he watched Selina Nashashibi that night. Ah, the power of the boob tube—and a boob queen.

I shifted my gaze to Glenn and had to laugh as he carefully tucked the bonus disc into his second burger, poking and prodding it meticulously into place with his finger. He seemed to be getting more animated under Burt's attentions. He was talking more than usual, and he kept adjusting his dark glasses with his free hand.

"See, me they know by name," he explained, "not by face. They know Mona set the fire, so she's the one they really focus on. It's not cool, but Muessa Junction's not big—once you get a rep, no one lets go of it." Then he choked—or was he snorting again?—and shook his burger-filled fist at Burt. "You know, one time I tried to tell people *I* set the fire. They didn't go for it. They knew the story and that was that. I could've talked till my face turned as blue as Mona's hair; people around here turned off their ears a long time ago. So I just shut my mouth. Best to live in the shadows, like Batman." He tapped the Dark Knight logo on his hat.

That incident had been harsh. All Glenn had been trying to do was spare me grief, but Principal Hood had that stick so firmly lodged up his butt he barely even acknowledged Glenn was talking to him. "I know what's what, young man," the old codger had declared like the pompous windbag he was. "With one's actions come consequences, and Miss Kent must learn that. Your interjection is inappropriate and untimely." Then he gave me detention for something so lame that I forget now what it was.

Glenn had been furious. That very day he renamed the principal the Joker and launched a tireless search for his archenemy's weak spot, that fatal flaw that mars all supervillains. He pledged that when he found it—and he would, mark his words!—he'd bring that Worker of Evil down in flames. No luck yet, though. So far, Glenn's nemesis had proven invincible.

As we ate, a line was forming at the door. All the tables and booths were stuffed with diners who barely spoke to each other, who just bit their burgers and chewed and chewed and chewed, looking about as alive as a tile floor. A subdued crowd ebbed and flowed at the front counter. All four registers were operating—*ching, ching, ching, ching!* Some teenagers near the edge of the crowd snickered and pointed at a kid who'd stuck straws up his nose. *Gee, the excitement of being a teenager in Muessa*

Junction. The manager was starting to regulate the flow of people in and out of the restaurant. He had a clicker in his hand like they use at amusement parks to count Ferris wheel riders. It was a typical lunchtime scene in Muessa Junction. Most of the town's businesses depended on student clientele, so when the university closed for the summer and the students and professors fled to cooler places, there wasn't much work to do. Bored, hot, and hungry, Junctioners congregated in air-conditioned restaurants—fast-food joints, that is. Everyone in this town was as hooked on burgers and fries as I was, and we had eight separate fast-food chains feeding our addiction and keeping the town afloat. It seemed like every other building was painted red, white, and yellow, with meal-deal posters in the windows and vents spewing fryer fumes skyward. The grease-tinted air currents cycled through the town as regularly as dull-eyed customers cycled through the restaurant doors.

Too bad Frizzbeard hadn't cycled out yet. He was getting creepy. This must be my day to attract creeps.

I dropped the fry I'd been about to eat. Suddenly it grossed me out. I had to get out of here, out of this packed restaurant, out of this bizarro town as fast as humanly possible. Meaning to grab another napkin to wipe my slick fingers, I accidentally picked up Burt's crinkled piece of paper. The Texas address was scrawled in chicken-scratch handwriting, but the back had a bunch of commercial printing on it:

It was a date page from a word-of-the-day desk calendar. Aha! No wonder Burt spoke like he'd swallowed a dictionary. Use a new word three times and it's yours, or so the saying goes. Clearly Burt was going for exclusive ownership of "plethora."

I certainly had a plethora of problems, and Frizzbeard wasn't going to let me forget it. Couldn't he let a girl eat in peace? The clown didn't even look away like people are supposed to when they make eye contact with a stranger. That was the rule, and everyone knew it. *Obviously I see you, old man.* The guy had no manners. I wished I had that sticker that decorated Binny's cash register: **Earth is full. Go home.**

Thinking of Binny made me think about our talk the day before. I would know when the time was right, he'd said. When the time was right for what?

The low drone of muffled voices was getting deeper as the crowd continued to grow. A loud buzz behind me announced a new batch of nuggets in the fryer. A squatty flattopped boy in a red, white, and yellow striped uniform scuttled past us and pushed into the crowd toward the kitchen. A second buzz signaled new fries. Another squatty flattop scuttled past. Now a faint *r-r-r* of sirens buzzed through the glass window next to me. No squatty flattopper scuttled to answer that call. The siren grew louder as it came closer.

Time for *what*? To stand up for myself? How? By whacking my skateboard into the shins of everyone who stared at me like I was some loser? By grabbing every Junctioner I met by the collar and shouting in their faces, "Snap out of it, you mindless drone! Find something more exciting to do than stare at me while you chew your cud!" Oh, this was so frustrating! No way could I take on the whole town, I knew that. Nobody around here would listen. Then I considered Frizzbeard. Maybe I could take on *one* guy. . . . But what would I do? What would I say?

R-r-r-r . . . Nobody else seemed to register the siren.

I had to start somewhere, though. And Frizzbeard was really pushing it.

R-r-r-r-r . . .

He was still staring. . . .

R-r-r-r-r-r . . .

I shot him the Stink Eye. . . .

R-r-r-r-r-r . . . !

Still staring . . .

R-r-r-r-r-r—!

"That's it!" Time to take care of business. I was finally going to speak up, and he *was* going to listen. I threw down my chewed-up straw, rose to my full five feet, and aimed a bumper stickerism straight at him: "The more people I meet, the more I like my dog!"

Frizzbeard's squinchy expression twisted, like, *Who, me?*

Yeah, you!

The sirens roared louder. The muffled drone ceased

and heads turned my way. Now I was standing on the plastic bench. "Next time you think you're perfect, try walking on water!"

One more step and I was on the table, taking aim at the entire now-silent restaurant. The sirens lodged between my ears as I hollered, "My job is to comfort the disturbed and disturb the comfortable!"

Every head was turned my way. Glenn's mouth hung open, half-chewed apple pie wadded to one side. And Burt, he was . . . peeking up my skirt! I smacked his black-haired head.

R-r-r!-R!-R!-R-r-r . . . A blazing red fire truck zipped past the window.

I spotted the squatty flattopped manager hustling around the counter and pushing toward me to stop the show. But my boots quickly clomped back to the ground on their own. I was done anyway. The skin above Frizzbeard's fuzz was fire engine red. And not a single cow was chewing in the whole place. I'd made them listen, all right. Take that, Muessa Junction!

4

Pop!

Pop!

Crack!

Breaking glass.

Voices shouting. Daddy shouting. Me shouting. "I can't see! Daddy, Daddy! Where are you, Daddy? I can't see you! Daddy!"

Pop! Pop! Crack!

R-r-r-r-r . . .

Where is Glenn . . . ?

R-r-r-r-r . . .

I can't see . . . !

R-r-r-r-r . . .
Sirens! Stop the sirens!
Beep, beep, beep!
Stop the beeps!
Beep, beep—

BANG! I flinched as a golf cart crashed into a bench right next to me. Distracted by the flashback that must have been sparked by my explosion at lunch, I'd wandered onto the mayor's golf course after running from the restaurant. The turf in front of City Hall was nothing but dirt and weeds, but our mayor putted on it twice a day because, as everyone knows, successful businessmen putt, and Muessa Junction mayors were always successful businessmen, and twice a day was always better than once.

Mayor Klunken hurled cusswords at me from his rumpled cart. I barely heard him. I'd slapped my hands over my ears to block out the stuck cart horn—*beeeeeeeep!*—and was already bolting down the street. He didn't run after me, but he didn't need to—I was being chased by something I could never see.

5

Running from the mayor, I cut over to Nugget Street, a road that eventually spits out at my house. I'd cruised that route on my skateboard a million times before—the bus stop, Burger King, the public library, Taco Bell, the fire-house, Jack in the Box. . . . This time, though, the scenery seemed different. The paint on the buildings was brighter, the logos more crisp, the VALUE MENU!!! signs more in focus. The sidewalk had a little give to it and a lot less lit-ter. I think the heat was somehow lighter, less intense. And the usually stale, filmy air smelled faintly floral, like Mar-garita was nearby. I even had an urge to skip. Being that my usual mood was tolerant bordering on pissy, I felt a little silly. Good silly. Happy silly. All because I'd stood up and made myself heard instead of clamming up and skulking out. Weird, but hey, whatever floats your boat, Skipper. Riding this rush sure beat dwelling on the fiery flashback Mayor Klunken had snapped me out of.

At my house, I took the cement steps up to my porch two at a time. I needed a new shirt before heading over to Dante's. I'm not a big fan of ketchup stains on my chest. This pit stop would just be a quick in-and-out, I didn't even pause at the neighbor's fence to throw a dirt clod at crotchety Mrs. Teaburtle's Dalmation. She's always letting him poop in our yard.

When I flung open the door, my dad surprised me by being right in front of me, sitting on a rickety bar stool, sucking a lime Otter Pop.

He threw his arms wide. "Mona! You're home!"

I stepped back against the door. "Hi?" My dad's normal location when I came home, if I came home at all during the day, was on the couch, zoned out on some TV rerun. But then, today wasn't a normal day; it was the eleventh. "Were you watching the door?"

"I been waiting for you."

I almost looked behind me to see who he was talking to. "Me? Why?"

"Because you're my Mona and it's our big day." He hopped off his bar stool, then jammed the Otter Pop into his mouth. His hands free, he carried the stool over to the breakfast bar that separated the kitchen from the living room. A tall stack of torn Swedish Meatball Supreme boxes wobbled ominously on the peeling, yellowed bar. Waiting to be crushed below it was a neatly stacked wall of cream soda cans, maybe three cans high and half a dozen wide.

I took a few steps into the living room. Something wasn't right.

As my dad carried on some unintelligible one-sided conversation through his ice-pop cork, I scanned the room. Then I realized what was wrong: It was sunny—inside my house.

Over behind the futon, the front window was wide open, the gray blinds raised high and the screen completely missing. The blinds on the kitchen windows were raised, too, their screens also missing. This had to be the first direct sunlight this room had seen in just about forever. I turned to the kitchen. A broom with all kinds of cobwebby, linty gook in its bristles leaned against the stove, and next to that was a bucket of black water with a grungy sponge floating on top. The few feet of kitchen floor visible around the corner of the bar was light blue instead of gray. I smelled lemons.

"Thought I'd do a little spring cleaning." My dad offered me an Otter Pop, the top plastic already neatly trimmed off. Louie-Bloo Raspberry. I always trashed the Louies as soon as I opened a box—raspberry-flavored food should not be blue. Dad must've gone out and bought a box himself.

I took the ice pop from his hand. "The house looks great, Dad. What is that, a vacuum cleaner? I didn't know we had a vacuum cleaner."

"We didn't. I borrowed it from Mrs. Teaburtle next door. A lovely woman. And that dog of hers, pure sunshine, nose to tail." He zipped back to the kitchen, where he opened the refrigerator and took out two plastic cereal bowls loaded with tiny gray lumps. Toothpicks stuck out of each one. "I thought we'd have a snack while we wait."

"Wait for what?"

"To watch our interview. It'll be a good one, I can tell. Better than last year's. Selina Nasha . . . nashas . . . shelibi . . . that pretty reporter lady was way better than Van Deacon. His teeth are fake."

"Dad, the interview won't be on for"—I checked my watch—"four hours, at least."

"Yeah, well, I was thinking maybe we can play a game till then. How about Chutes and Ladders? You love Chutes and Ladders."

"When I was six. I don't think we even have it anymore."

"Oh. Well, let's bake cookies, then. You like cookies. Everyone likes cookies."

"Cookies?" I looked around the sunny room, at the broom, at the blue linoleum and the digusting water. Dad must've spent hours on his hands and knees. And I can't even guess how long it took to dig all those meatballs out of the frozen dinners and poke toothpicks in every one. I wonder what happened to the supreme Swedish noodles. "Yeah, okay, we can bake cookies. Do you know how?"

"I thought you did."

"Why would I know how to bake cookies?"

"Because you're Mona."

What was that, a compliment? If it was, it was pretty weak. But if it wasn't, then I didn't know what it was. I swear, there were times I wished I could peer through my dad's ears and see what was going on in that brain of his. Most of the time, though, it was just easier to pretend he didn't even have one.

"I guess we can figure it out, Dad. Where are the chips? There's a recipe on the package." Glenn and I ate chocolate chips when we watched the late-night cartoon channel. We had a pact to only eat a chip at a time, so one bag lasted two or even three shows.

Dad set the meatball bowls on the counter and started patting his front jeans pockets and then his back pockets and then looking around the floor by his feet. "Chips, chips . . ." Then he held up his hands, empty palms facing me, and shrugged.

"You didn't buy any chocolate chips?" I asked.

"Why would I buy chocolate chips?"

"For cookies." This might be one of those no-brain moments. "Forget it. We'll just eat the meatballs." I took a bowl and walked to the futon. I had no intention of watching the interview—with or without him—but I wasn't about to pass up a spontaneous father-daughter day. I'd finish my Louie, eat tiny meat rocks on sticks for a while, we'd talk about . . . I don't know . . . something, and then I'd bolt before the six o'clock news.

Dad worked the last piece of his Otter Pop out of the plastic and into his mouth and carefully tucked the empty wrapper into his pocket. Then he brought over his meatballs and sat next to me. "This'll be great."

"Yeah. This was a good idea."

He put a meatball into his mouth. "I just wish your dear momma was here to share this feast with us." He stopped chewing for a moment, and his eyes started unfocusing. *Shoot*. But then, just as quickly, he shook his head, smiled at me, and finished chewing. "Tomorrow will be even better. When's the last time you and me stepped out together, huh? You'll love it. Folks will come up to us and shake our hands. We'll be like movie stars. Everybody will know us. It's like taking off a disguise: Suddenly people know who you really are"—he leaned over and playfully poked my nose—"which is a very important person. People like important people."

"Not on this planet."

"Yes, they do. You never come with me, so you just don't know. You'll love it, Mona, you'll see. You'll feel like part of a big family."

"A big dysfunctional family."

"Now, now . . . an empty glass of water is always halfway full. Remember that."

"But, Dad—"

"*Butts* are for cigarettes, baby. I'll make sure no one overlooks you. Just leave it to Daddy." He reached out and ruffled my hair.

I bolted to my feet. "You know what, Dad? I gotta go." I was on the stairs quicker than it takes to flick a cigarette, butt and all. "Glenn is probably worried about me. I just came home to change my shirt."

"Wait, what about the interview?"

I hollered over my shoulder, "You'll have to watch it without me."

"But you have to be here, Mona. We need to celebrate as a family. Mona?" His voice grew fainter as I reached the top. "I can't watch the interview alone. Please stay. Mona? Mona! I need you!" I turned into my room, bumper stickers everywhere. "You're the whole reason we're famous!"

I slammed my door.

Dogs are a bunch of kiss-up fakers. They have everyone thinking they're all cute and cuddly and obedient so that you'll give them a pat and a bone, but they're not. Mrs. Teaburtle's Dalmation is a prime example. Pure sunshine, my heiny. Pure pain, I'd say. His behavior today only proved that to me. There I was, minding my own business, climbing down my own tree out of my own stupid window, when that spotted beast let fly with a barrage of barking from his side of the fence.

"Shhh! Shut up, Snookums. Shhh!" I should've saved my breath. Of course my dad heard the noise and looked out the front door. Stupid dog. I had to drop past the last few branches and run like a thief. Whether Dad saw me or not, I couldn't say.

I found Glenn and Burt in Dante's perched on the edge of the futon, with Ozzy Osbourne screeching something about crazy trains in the background. They were leaning over a Superman comic that lay open on the coffee table. Burt's feet rested on my skateboard, rolling it absently left, right, left, right. That board sure would've been handy a few minutes ago. Wheels always make for quicker get-aways.

"Howdy, boys."

Burt looked up and hopped to his feet, nearly taking a header thanks to my board at his feet. That kid was a disaster waiting to happen. "Mona! See, Glenn? She didn't run away for good. I told you."

"Well, well." Glenn leaned back on the futon and crossed his arms. "Our spunky heroine is full of surprises today."

"What, you wrote me off? Silly mortal, it takes more than a bad beard to bring down this girl." I raised both my arms and flexed. "I am invincible."

Glenn shook his head. "I swear, Monalisa Kent, if one person survived a nuclear holocaust, it would be you."

"Me and the cockroaches."

"They have my sympathy. You do realize you've

71

blown your cover, don't you? The Workers of Evil will know your blue disguise now."

I reached up and stretched a few strands of my blue bangs forward, crossing my eyes so I could look at them. I let go and shrugged. Blue was a depressing color anyway. "My dad's interview would've taken care of that for me. At least this way I was the one who pulled the trigger." I moved around to his side of the table and sat down on it, my knees touching his. "So, wha—"

"Hey, that's a new comic!"

"Sorry." I leaned to my left while he pulled the comic free. "So, what do you think? Should I feel humiliated?"

"I did."

"You? Why?"

"The manager made us leave. I wasn't even finished. Were you finished, Burt?"

Burt shrugged. "Cold French fries are yuck anyway."

"See," I said, "he's fine. Don't worry, Glenn. If I got anyone blackballed, it's me."

Burt sat back down. "How'd you know to say that stuff?"

I pointed to my bumper-stickered boot. "Some people read comic books, I read bumper stickers. I have about a million memorized."

"Believe it," Glenn said. "She's got a line for everything. And it's usually not what you want to hear."

"I beg your pardon." I crossed my arms. "Someday you'll thank me for keeping you grounded. Thin skin is for the weak. Would you rather I quote those awful soliloquies Mrs. Kaplan made us memorize last year?"

Glenn didn't reply for a moment; he just sat there. I was about to say something else when he suddenly threw his arms wide and bellowed, "To be or not to be . . . !"

I pulled back in surprise. Glenn never bellowed, certainly not in front of other people. "What was that about?"

"Did it make you uncomfortable?"

"Yeah, it made me uncomfortable. Do you think you could holler in my face any louder, Hamlet?"

He looked at me for another second and then smiled—only it was a weird smile, one that didn't touch the rest of his face. With a lumbering jerk, he stood up, stuck his tongue way out, and grabbed his throat like he was gagging.

I fell backward on the table. His gut was right in front of me.

Clutching his throat and gagging some more, he stumbled left and right a few times, then flopped to the floor, where he continued to thrash and gag in what had to be some kind of bizarre death scene. Only he looked more like a fish on hot coals than a dying Shakespeare guy. Now *that's* humiliating.

But Burt was laughing and slapping the futon like this was the funniest thing he'd ever seen. So Glenn kept flapping around on the floor.

"God, Glenn, what are you doing?" I said. This floor

flopping was unnerving, maybe as unnerving as my dad's floor scrubbing was. What was up with guys and floors today? "Glenn . . . someone will see you. . . . Glenn . . ." I stood up and nudged one of his flailing feet. "Glenn, I think I hear Chet."

Glenn froze his body, his neck arched so that his dark glasses pointed at the Hole. Sure enough, Chet walked out of the tiny back room with Margarita trailing behind. She stopped when she saw her son scrambling up from the floor. "Paquito, are you okay?"

"I'm fine, Mom." Glenn dusted off the back of his shorts and sat back down.

I lowered my voice so they wouldn't hear me over the Ozzy tune. "I thought I'd have to call 911. What was that?"

He motioned me off the table, and when I got up, he laid his comic book on it again, leaned in, and started reading. When Burt saw him turn a page, he quickly leaned in and started reading, too. Burt tried to peek back at the page he'd missed, but Glenn kept his hand firmly on it. They sat there, the both of them, leaning over the comic, moving their lips in unison.

I stood there waiting for Glenn's answer while Margarita directed Chet over to one of the cabinets and started pulling out pink towels and stacking them in his arms. When the fluffy pink tower reached the wooden peg in Chet's eyebrow, Margarita turned him by his shoulders, lined him up with the Hole, and then marched him forward and into it.

Their exit left a weird silence. It was obvious I wasn't going to get an answer, so I tried to think of something else to say so that I wouldn't look so lame just standing there, ignored. "Glenn, you wouldn't believe my dad—" Glenn shushed me with a raised "please wait" finger. He didn't even look up, just raised his finger.

"This is a good part," he said into the comic.

"Well, pardon me for living." I leaned over and yanked up the edge of his great literature, pulled a new issue of *Trash Tats* from underneath, then let his comic fall flat again. Then I stepped over to the black leather chair at the head of the coffee table. The chair was positioned with its back to the street door, so I could see the whole shop in a glance. I settled into the soft bucket seat, put my booted feet up on the table, and opened my magazine with a full-wrist snap. I could immerse myself in the written word, too, thank you very much. And I wouldn't have to move my lips while I did it.

People came and went throughout the afternoon, but it wasn't until dark that traffic in Dante's really picked up. I swear, the Glenns' tattoo parlors had to be the most energetic places in this whole clueless town. Dante's was a lot smaller than the Pink Cloud, so whenever I got bored with issues of *Trash Tats,* I just dropped the magazine into my lap and watched whichever customer was the most interesting. I had my pick since there were no drapes to pull around Tuck's chairs like in the Pink Cloud. At Dante's, tattooing wasn't done in private, no matter which body part was involved.

For the longest time, I watched Wally work on the shoulder of a tanned lifeguard who sat there like a stone statue. The guy had driven three hours from some swanky beach town on the coast just for a tattoo from Dante's. He was getting a monochrome portrait of his three-year-old daughter, and Wally had told him that if he moved, the child might end up with a mustache—or worse. From that moment on, the dad didn't move a muscle, not when the needle first touched his skin or even while he talked to Wally about his little girl, who could already swim in light surf and resuscitate a stuffed doll. I tried hard, but I didn't see the man's lips move, yet every sweet, proud word he uttered about the girl was loud and clear. It was like having a ventriloquist in the shop—a proud papa ventriloquist.

When the lifeguard left, his chair didn't even get cold before Wally had another guy in it who wanted his name tattooed across his muscled chest in Gothic letters. The guy's buddy sat in Chet's chair and ordered the same treatment of his own name. They both wore red bandanas on their heads. A third guy with a red bandana sat on the sidewalk outside and smoked, his head swiveling left and right as he scanned the streets. He looked like a thug at a tennis match. The pizza Tuck had ordered earlier arrived only a few minutes after the bandana boys sat down, but

Tuck wouldn't let Chet or Wally stop to eat. He wanted those customers done and out fast.

Tuck stood in the doorway the whole time they were there, his head swiveling left and right just like the smoker's. Glenn and Burt didn't seem to notice Tuck's edginess, but I did. I started asking Tuck stuff to lighten the tension.

"Want some pizza, Tuck?"

"No."

"Want me to put on different music?"

"No."

"Where'd Margarita go?"

"Out."

"When will she be back?"

"Later."

"Who's the Guy?"

"No comment."

Shoot. Thought I might trip him up there. Can't blame a girl for trying. One day one of those Glenns will crack on the Guy thing.

Eventually I ran out of questions and just went back to watching the bandana boys try to look tough through their pain.

None of these people noticed me watching them. When you're getting a tattoo, your focus is all on the needle digging into you. It was the same with people trying to decide which tattoo to get. They were always so intent on the pictures in the portfolios or taped on the metal walls that the president could walk in and they wouldn't notice. A tattoo parlor is a great place to people watch without being watched by people.

As the shop started bustling, Chet, Wally, and I took turns playing DJ with the music. I liked the more melodic stuff, while Chet and Wally just liked songs with a lot of pounding and high-pitched guitar solos. I ran a few fetch-it errands for them here and there, but mostly I just hung back and took in the action.

Glenn and Burt worked their way through Glenn's "greatest superhero hits" comic book box. I said a few things to Glenn now and then, but not much, because he wouldn't really answer me—"Want a Pepsi?" "No."— that sort of stuff. Mostly he stayed pouty and lectured Burt on the finer points of superhero literature.

Glenn's moodiness was sure getting extreme lately, even for him. But he was my oldest friend, so I figured I should try to cut him some slack on his attitude. After all, July eleventh was a bad date for him, too. The heat from the fire had seared his optic nerves, making them super-sensitive to light, and there was no fixing them. Not that his macho streak would ever let him admit that he cared a flying fig about his eyes or the eleventh. Especially these days, with his conversation consisting mainly of impatient snorts and cranky comments.

Now and then, when nothing else interesting was going on, my mind wandered back to my tiptoe-through-the-tulips walk home this afternoon. I'd felt so much lighter, like I'd dumped out a backpack of rocks I'd been unknowingly schlepping around. It was a good feeling to let something out for once instead of pushing it deeper. An adrenaline rush, even. I couldn't think too long about this, though, because this train of thought kept leading me to the same place the walk did: my living room, with my dad, his open windows, and his lemon-scented sunshine. Here the man was finally letting out the gloom, and what did I do? I left him sitting in his sunshine with nothing but a bowl of meatballs and a clock ticking down to Selina's segment on the weekend news hour. Some daughter I am. But I couldn't stay. I just couldn't. And anyway, by now the show was long over, so the damage was done and that was that.

It got easier to keep my mind off of my dad when Potter Pete came in. He was the guy I'd nearly leveled before lunch. It was hard to think of anything too serious with him around. If Dante's was the last refuge for the original thinkers in this cookie-cutter town, Potter was the king of the refugees.

Potter claimed he got his nickname from potted meat. What *that* was I didn't know, but it sounded awful. Maybe he sold it on his meat truck. I saw him sometimes, on duty, cruising the streets like the ice cream man, only Potter Pete hawked beef shank and mutton instead of Fudgsicles. It seemed goofy to me to buy filet mignon from a guy in a run-down refrigerated truck with an I SAW ELVIS MAKING CROP CIRCLES bumper sticker (care of me, of course), but people did it. It was convenient, I guess, like pizza delivery. Folks came rushing out of houses up and down the street like dogs to a whistle when they heard Pete's Meat Wagon blaring Elvis hits through its staticky loudspeakers. The town's lardy air further muffled the tunes, resulting in a noise so distorted that Potter's "Hunk o' Hunk o' Burning Love" marathon last month had left half the town humming "hubba hubba burps 'n' crud" for days.

When Potter wasn't cruising in his meat wagon, he was working on a full-body tattoo. Total Technicolor—no generic black ink for him. Sometimes I worried that he had mad cow disease or something else that makes people loopy, though, because that kind of body art requires tons of sessions—hours and hours of painful needle-scratching—and serious cash. His back art alone took thousands of dollars and nearly three months for Tuck to draw and color. But Potter said it was worth every pin-pricking minute, because now he had his own personal baseball diamond lodged between his shoulder blades. Potter Park, he called it. He even had half-inch-high base-ball players on the field, twisting and stretching along with his back muscles.

Hey, it made him happy.

That wasn't all, though. Not by a long shot. Above the scoreboard, spanning the top of Potter's shoulders and stretching down each arm to his wrists, was a keyboard covered with half-inch jitterbuggers. There was even a half-inch Elvis in miniature blue suede shoes. Sometimes I'd catch Potter fingering the tattooed keys like he was playing "Jailhouse Rock" or "Take Me Out to the Ballgame" or something.

As soon as Burt saw Potter's arms, he clapped his hands and scurried over and pretended to play piano on one, belting out "Mary Had a Little Lamb" and dancing a jig. Potter shot me an expression like, "Who is this kid?" I just shrugged. I figured that Burt would have to go home soon anyway. His uncle George was cool enough, but allowing his thirteen-year-old nephew to pull an all-nighter would be asking a lot of the old cameraman.

The bigger question, I thought, was whether Burt would fit through the door of his uncle's house. The kid's pockets were bulging. He'd completely stuffed them with tattoo templates because he wanted to think on which was his favorite. Not that anyone would ink the kid. That was a crime worse than buying booze for underage drinkers, and the evidence was permanent. The law said a person had to be eighteen to get a tattoo, period. Underagers came into Dante's and the Pink Cloud all the time, thinking they could persuade Tuck or Margarita to ink them on the sly. Not in this lifetime. The Glenns weren't interested in relocating their tattoo empire to the Big House.

What I couldn't figure out was, what was with all the impatience, anyway? If the underagers would just chill out a few years, they could have all the ink they wanted. This wasn't one of those backward states where tattooing was totally illegal. In those states, if you wanted a tattoo, you had to rely on the underground tattoo circuit—and you never knew what unregulated tattooists were doling out. Smudged tattoos by amateurs were the least of your worries. You had to worry about dirty, nonsterile needles in the hands of quick-money scammers or even well-meaning wannabes. And that was just asking for hepatitis, pus-oozing infections, or nasty scars. A lot of people just couldn't wait, though, and those were the kinds of customers Tuck turned away regardless of age. Impulse tattoos ended up being the most hated tattoos. Yet they were so common that licensed tattooists made big-time cash covering them up with larger, nicer tattoos. High-class doctors made even more dough lasering them off completely. None of Tuck's creations would ever see a laser, not if he could help it, anyway. Margarita, on the other hand, she depended on impulse tattoos on her side of the Hole. Trendy tattoos are all about the Moment, and the Moment is what the Pink Cloud sold.

Not that I thought Burt even wanted a tattoo. When Glenn first pulled out the flash book of templates to entertain him, the kid had freaked out over the colorful design sheets, getting spastic with delight at each flip of the page. And Professor Glenn was putting on quite a show, going on and on about each image like he was our old art teacher, Mr. Yuri, using words like *symmetry* and *symbolism*. Burt hung on every fifty-cent word.

"That used to be my favorite." Glenn was pointing

out a skull that had flames shooting out of the eye sockets. "But I'm not into skulls anymore. There's really nothing to them once you get over the hype—just bones and eye sockets. Now I like this one a lot." Batman devouring balls of fire, red and orange flickers in his eyes. "The Dark Knight, king of all superheroes. A human who made himself superhuman." Glenn sighed like a schoolgirl with a crush. I had to stifle a giggle. "But then, this one's pretty cool—"

"That's the trouble with tattoos, you know," I interrupted. "What's cool one day is boring the next. Anyway, how do you know which tattoo is the real you? Pick the wrong one and you're sorry for life. None of that for me. I can pull out my belly button ring, I can't wipe off a tattoo."

Glenn ignored me. I could tell what he was doing by the way he tilted his head to put the bill of his Batman hat between me and his dark glasses. Burt didn't seem to hear me.

Fine. I moved from my bucket seat by the door to a bar stool made of hubcaps and old fence posts on the opposite side of the room. It had just been vacated by a mullet-headed guy with a KISS T-shirt who had scanned portfolios for more than an hour without making up his mind. There, I grabbed a grapefruit from a bowl on the counter. Not to eat, to practice. Tuck always kept a supply of them around so that he and Chet and Wally could keep their needling skills sharp. The curvy shape and weird

83

texture of the rind made grapefruits perfect stand-ins for human body parts.

I'd recently started needling fruit for fun. Maybe someday I'd open a parlor of my own, if I got good enough. My guidance counselor would be pleased to know I had a fallback career if being a professional bumper sticker writer didn't work out. My shop wouldn't be anything like Dante's, though. That was too Tuck. It wouldn't be like the Pink Cloud, either. Too Margarita. Mine would be all Mona.

Whatever that was.

I was concentrating on drawing an outline when a loud *bang!* on the counter next to me sent my needle ripping across the rind.

I whipped my head up and locked eyes with a yellow smiley face. I instantly recognized the yellow graphic and the HAVE A NICE DAY below it as the image on Roy's favorite T-shirt. I craned my neck up. Yep, Roy. The guy was six foot six and skinny as an ostrich neck. Elbows and knees jutted every which way, and his pointy goatee poked out from his otherwise baby face like a gelled black beak. His easy smile and playful eyes softened the angles a bit, but still, he must stick out of a crowd like a stork on stilts. That had to be murder.

"Sorry, Mona." He pounded his palm against the side of the open box he'd plunked onto the counter. The wrinkles in his knuckles were permanently stained with grease or some other gunky car juice. "I didn't know it would make that much noise."

I doubted that. Nothing Roy did was quiet. "I can fix it." I wiped the grapefruit's juicing slash dry on his thrashed black jeans, then turned on my needle and went back to work.

"Glad to be of service." He leaned against the counter and checked out my grapefruit. "Hey, hey! It's surfing Gumby!" He thumped my shoulder encouragingly. "Fine draftsmanship."

Shoot. It was supposed to be a girl on a skateboard, not a surfing Gumby. I made a face at Roy, but truth be told, I did see Gumby now that he'd shouted it out. I might as well have a sense of humor about it. "Hey, Burt," I called out, "you're a tattoo."

Again Burt didn't hear me. Again Glenn ignored me. *Whatever.*

Instead of moving on to someone more interesting, Roy leaned down closer to my grapefruit. His breathing was loud so close to my ear. I shifted away a little. A girl needs her space.

"You know . . ." He pulled a dog-eared paperback out of his back pocket and riffled the pages. Stopping on a page near the end, he looked at my fruit, then at his book, then at my fruit again. "Yep, that's what I thought." He pointed a grease-nailed finger at my skateboarder. "Shading the upper curvature would create a perception of depth regardless of the beholder's angle. Have you considered that?"

Roy had taken freshman art classes at the college on his days off from his family's auto wrecking yard. He popped off with the goofiest things now.

"I was just about to," I said. "Thanks."

"And you could deepen the color of his left leg to make his forward stride appear more dynamic."

"Okay. I'll do that."

"After that, just let him tell you what he needs next."

"I'll let him tell me."

"Attagirl. You're on the right track, Mona." He thumped my shoulder again. "The key is to keep pushing your comfort threshold."

I don't think so. My comfort threshold had been pushed around enough today. "I will push it. Thank you."

"Anytime. Just holler if you need us." He held the book next to his little boy face and flashed a cheesy grin, like he was posing for a picture in a photo booth. Then he stuffed it back into his pocket. "Hey"—he lowered his voice to how normal people speak and pointed at Burt— "who's the kid?"

"Some stray Glenn's adopting. His name's Burt."

"Well, they're wasting their time with that portfolio." He grabbed the Horsepower, Ltd., binder from the counter and walked over to the futon. "Glenn, show him this one."

Glenn shoved the thick leather binder away. "He

doesn't want to see cars. We've still got four superheroes design sets to go through."

But Burt grabbed Horsepower from Roy with both tiny hands. "Cars are cool."

"Fine," Glenn said, "look at cars."

As Burt flipped through the pages of hot rod and dragster tattoo templates, Roy pulled a blue racquetball out of his hip pocket and started squeezing it. I swear, Roy's pants were like a clown car—you never knew what he was going to pull out of his pocket next. Catching Burt's puzzled expression, Roy explained that ball squeezing would make his forearms more defined. He hated being so beanpoley. "If you have people looking at your body art, you should have a body worth looking at." Last week he had a Thighmaster going. Pretty brave thing for a guy to do in a tattoo parlor. I swear, Dante's attracted all the misfits in this stale town. Maybe that was one of the reasons I felt so comfortable there.

What was weird about Roy's obsession with pumping up was that he didn't have any body art to look at—not yet, anyway. He'd been coming in since he turned eighteen last year, but he couldn't make up his mind about what tattoo to get. And I had a feeling that taking that art class had only made him pickier. I almost won him over last week, though, with my idea to run a racetrack up one leg, across his butt, then back down the other leg, with all kinds of flashy hotrods and hairpin turns along the way. Oh, the temptation that had flickered in his eyes over that idea! He was obsessed with cars. Ultimately, though, he decided against the racetrack. Just as well, I guess—the diciest turns would've been hidden from public view anyway.

The smell of French fries caught my attention. The town usually reeked of fries, but it seemed stronger all of a sudden. I sniffed around to locate the source, then fished in the box Roy had left beside me. It was full of cracked rearview mirrors. Mixed in with them, though, were several grease-spotted carry-out bags jammed with burgers and nuggets, onion rings and fries, and dozens of mustard and ketchup packets.

Food runs were a nightly staple at Dante's. Tonight Roy had done the honors. Only, he forgot to dole out the goods. I guess a bunch of car tattoos was more important than food. Since I wasn't doing anything but butchering fruit and wasting oxygen, I'd finish his job. Unbagging the food, I hollered out each item, then hucked it to whoever claimed it first. They tossed back coins and airplane-folded dollar bills. I didn't bother to count the cash. The Dante's honor system was impeccable. I just stuffed the money into one of the empty bags. Each night, the regular who lost at Rock, Paper, Scissors would grab the previous night's moneybag and duck out on the late-night munchies run.

With all the food served, I scanned the room. It was clear of customers for the moment. Seizing the opportunity, I quickly rolled the cash-filled sack closed and dragged my bar stool across the room. Using the stool as a ladder, I wedged the loot bag behind the face mask of what Roy had dubbed the Plymouth Knight. It was a seven-foot-tall doorstop standing guard at the front entrance. Propping open the door during business hours, the sentry weighed several hundred pounds at least, and stood at attention on a wheeled plank. It was named in honor of Roy's pride and joy: his flashy candy red Plymouth Prowler roadster. To be honest, from a distance the knight looked like a pile of junk. But up close you could see that it was a suit of armor made from welded car parts. It had "tattoos" painted on each arm and a **Tattoos for the Damned** bumper sticker plastered across its chest plate. That was my contribution. Roy and Glenn were the ones who made him. Glenn had just discovered my dad's old welding tools, and Roy had just decided he was placed on Earth to be an Artist. Plus he had an endless supply of metal, thanks to Pennyworth Auto Wrecking. He and Glenn got inspired to combine their new hobbies and create a suit of arms after watching a Monty Python movie about knights who banged coconut shells together. And it went with the medieval mural on Dante's ceiling. The two new partners set up their stuff on the sidewalk in front of Dante's and started welding away one day, sparks shooting everywhere. They'd also tried to weld a horse for the brave knight, but it always came out looking like an oversize cat, or a giraffe, or one time even a rhino. Eventually they gave up and turned their car art to more functional things, like hubcap chairs and bumper lamps. They didn't bother making couches, though—there was no topping my dad's now-classic futon designs. Back in the day when Muessa Junction was a proud cog in the world of furniture manufacturing, people would fly here from all over the world just to have my dad design and weld them futons. That's how Margarita tells it, anyway. My dad's metal futon frame stylings were said to evoke birds in flight, cats on the prowl, sharks circling their prey. They were all about motion and strength—two things that no longer had anything to do with Mac Kent or Muessa Junction.

With the food run complete and our tummies happy, we fell into our usual evening routine. The radio laid down a pulsing layer of background noise. Above the bass line a comforting buzz droned as needles etched away. Across the room, Chet was working on a skuzzy old biker who wanted a skuzzier old SANDRA FOREVER tattoo changed to SANTA FOREVER. Every few minutes, Chet would turn his head and spit a stream of tobacco juice over his shoulder into a spittoon fashioned from a muffler. A few feet over, Wally was having his temper tested by a skittish gang-banger-wannabe kid with bandanas wrapped around each thigh. The kid kept climbing into the chair and hopping out again when Wally touched him with the needle. Wally's face kept getting redder and redder around his swirled tribal tattoo—I worried that the peg in his eyebrow might shoot out like a cork at any moment. Since I knew the kid had to be over eighteen to be getting a tattoo here, I figured he was older than he looked. He certainly wasn't braver than he looked. And I doubted that having a tattoo would make him any tougher.

Tuck was working the chair closest to me and the boys. He was grinding his needle into Potter's head, adding the words You Are Here next to an arrow in the middle of Potter's bull's-eye.

"It don't hurt much on the skull," Potter kept telling me. Which was proof enough to me that his mad cow disease was finally nearly full bloom. If I had a needle buzzing that close to my ear, I would have a stroke for sure. But Potter kept telling funny stories about the customers on his meat route, so maybe it really didn't hurt.

"I'm telling you," he said, "you will *not* believe what Principal Hood's old lady had going today. I swear, that woman is a throwback to better days in this town. There I am, cruising down Hashbrowne Road, right, and she comes traipsing out of her house in a gorilla suit. No joke! She walks right up to my truck like there's nothing out of the ordinary and asks me do I have any crocodile meat. Croc meat? You gotta be kidding me." He cracked up and the rest of us did, too. "'Mrs. Hood,' I tell her, 'I don't carry croc. I got some prime lamb, though. Will that work?' You know what she says to me? She says, 'Mr. Potter, this evening's theme is Jungle Safari, and I simply must procure a crocodile cutlet.' Then she talks me into getting on my cell phone and calling 'my esteemed colleagues' to see if they can score her any croc. And you know what? Barney in Mesa Villa can get me some. No joke! I swear on my filet mignon. So now she's postponing Jungle Safari night to next week when I can deliver croc cutlets. Tonight will be Barnyard Buffet instead. Lamb chops and ham hocks. Says she's got some 'dungarees and a lovely straw bonnet.' No joke!"

Tuck kept yelling stuff like "Shut up!" and "Stop laughing!" because Potter's yakking jaw made his head skin move. But Tuck was laughing just as much as we were, so he should've saved his breath. When Potter had an audience, there was no clamming him up.

Because of his meat route, Potter had stories about everyone in town. He could tell you who was dating who, who was cheating on who, and, of course, where the hottest girls lived. Not that they would date Potter. It would take a special kind of girl to date a twenty-five-year-old meat hawker with all-over body art. And the new bull's-eye wasn't likely to improve his social life any. Of course, that was just my opinion.

I had an idea. "Hey, Potter? Do you know some old guy with a frizzy beard?"

"You just described every male Junctioner over fifty. What else can you tell me?"

"That's it. Glenn? Do you remember anything about the guy at lunch? Glenn?" I turned to catch Glenn pulling the brim of his Batman hat lower over his dark glasses.

"Oh, I'm sorry, I didn't mean to disturb you, Your Highness. Burt, do you?"

"He didn't have any earlobes."

That earned Burt looks from everyone, even Mr. Minding My Own Business Under My Stupid Hat.

"No earlobes?" I said. "How does someone not have earlobes?"

"I don't know. He just didn't."

Burt was one weird kid. "Okay. No earlobes. Potter, is that enough?"

Potter was still staring at Burt like the little Q-tip had just sprouted an elephant's trunk. Eventually Potter shook his head, scoring him a forearm in the back from Tuck. "Stop moving!" Tuck bellowed.

"Sorry, Mona." Potter only moved his mouth this time. "I don't know anything about anyone's earlobes. Why do you want to know?"

Burt answered for me. "She totally yelled at the guy. Stood right up on her table at lunch and yelled bumper sticker stuff to make him stop staring at her."

I held my breath, wondering what they'd say about that.

"You stood on a table?" Potter asked.

"Uh-huh," I said.

"In a public place?" That was Roy.

"Yeah."

"And you yelled stuff?" That was Tuck.

"Only what needed to be said. People need to pull their heads back out where the sun shines."

Potter slapped his hand solidly on his thigh. "Well, whip me with a wet noodle. Tuck, our baby has finally unleashed on the world the spit and vinegar she usually reserves for us loved ones. I'm so proud." Potter pretended to wipe a tear from his eye, then leaned forward and shook my hand.

"Hold still!" Tuck barked. "Mona, what'd you yell?" He sounded like he might send me to my room, if I had one here.

I looked down at the sticker on my left boot: I GOT OUT OF BED FOR *THIS?* "Just stuff."

"She called him a dog," Burt said. "And then she said he could go drown himself."

"Burt! I never said that!"

Glenn laughed. "So much for eyewitness testimony."

"You're the last one to be talking about anyone's eyes," I snapped.

"Enough." Tuck was the law around here, so I shut up. Glenn didn't say anything else, either. "Well? Did it work? Did he leave you alone?"

"I don't know. I left."

"She bolted like a thief with the loot." Burt scrambled up onto the metal coffee table and posed like a runner on a gold sports trophy. A ticker-tape parade of flash templates spilled from his pockets. "Let's do it again, Mona. I want to try."

"No, you don't." Glenn tapped Burt's leg and pointed to another tattoo in his binder. This portfolio had photos of the Guy's amazing work. "Look at this one."

Burt followed orders, climbing down from the table and plopping down onto the futon. He scooped up his templates and crumpled them back into his pockets. When he focused on the page in front of him, he leaned in for a closer look. "Wow, that is cool."

I almost said something about distracting Glenn's fan club, but I caught myself. I didn't know what Tuck would do if I mouthed off after his warning, but I didn't want to find out. One time Tuck had made me polish the Plymouth Knight when he heard me cussing. Lucky for me, he left soon after and I talked Glenn into finishing the polish job—it would've taken me forever to do it. I didn't want to risk another polishing assignment, so I held my tongue this time. Besides, I was starting to feel kind of frazzled. Two greasy guys in maybe their thirties had just walked in, and one of them was whispering something in his friend's ear and pointing at me. The Postinterview Point Fest was beginning. Glenn had said I could survive a nuclear attack, but I wasn't so sure I would even make it through this day without melting down. Strangers were pointing at me and Tuck was frowning. Potter was giving me a tattooed thumbs-up and Burt was planning an encore. Glenn was disowning me, and Roy was . . .

I looked around for the walking megaphone. He'd moved from the stool next to me to the doorway, where he was going up on his tiptoes, then flat-footed again, up on his toes, then flat-footed again. He was working out his calves now, I guessed. The whole time his left arm laid across the Plymouth Knight's shoulders like an old pal and his eyes gazed out at the star bright sky.

"All the world's a stage. You just needed the right lighting," he said. I didn't know if he was talking to me or to the Plymouth Knight or to the stars he gazed up at. Or maybe he was gazing at the ruins of the plant across the street. I didn't know and didn't care anymore. My skin felt hot, and my temples were starting to ache. I climbed down from my hubcap bar stool and squeezed into the Hole for a soda from the mini fridge.

The coolness of the open refrigerator was soothing. I lingered in front of it, wasting electricity, I knew. I heard a light clip-clop coming closer from the Pink Cloud side of the Hole; then I smelled roses. A tiny hand settled in the middle of my back.

Margarita whispered in my ear, "I saw *tu padre* on the news, *Bebita*."

My back went ramrod straight.

Here we go, the first of the interview fallout. And it starts with Margarita. Lovely.

I felt Margarita's hand start to pull away, but then it stayed and began rubbing in little circles. I almost pulled away myself, but I didn't. Where would I go, home? Not until I had to. Who knows where my dad would be sitting in wait?

So I stood there, letting Margarita play wannabe momma. If she wanted to feel like she was soothing me, what did I care? I was That Monalisa Kent Girl. I'd survived flaming infernos. I'd survived ten years in a town where everyone hates me. I could survive a nuclear holocaust, for crying out loud. Certainly I could survive Margarita's mothering. As for surviving this awful day and the next few weeks or even months of interview fallout, well, I was invincible, wasn't I? Me and the cockroaches. I'd think of some way to deal with it. I wouldn't go down without a fight, not this time. If I had to shout from every tabletop in Muessa Junction to do it, I'd show this grudge-carrying town that I was done skulking away like some pathetic cockroach.

Tears pooled in the corners of my eyes. The red, white, and blue logo on the soda can in my hand started to ripple. Distant squeals of girls egging each other on in the Pink Cloud floated to my ears like voices under water. Margarita rested her chin on my shoulder. Her soft voice and beautiful accent stilled the red, white, and blue ripples. "*Ay, Bebita.* Each time you think you picked the last chili from your burrito, another chili appears."

I grimaced. The Juarez Family Food Wisdom had reared its moldy head. Margarita claimed to have inherited this unique way of viewing the world from her dear *mamita,* who knew two things: cooking and old wives' tales. She blended the two in a magical philosophy that had flavored all the Juarez women for generations. That was Margarita's story, anyway. I doubted, though, that Food Wisdom really had dog-paddled its way through the gene pool to Margarita. The woman couldn't cook beans worth beans, so the Food part wasn't her thing. And as for the Wisdom part, maybe *Mamita* had dished up insightful life advice, but Margarita's advice . . . well, that was as hard to swallow as her chimichangas.

Margarita whispered once again, this time with the intensity you'd expect from a Little Hulk. "A burnt tortilla makes a good hat, *Bebita*. Make yourself a hat." She clamped her hand on my head. "Make yourself a hat."

At that, I cracked a smile and relaxed. Maybe Margarita didn't have Food Wisdom, but the image of my own blueberry do crowned by a charred flour yarmulke sure hit the spot.

6

Sunday, July twelfth. The morning after.

This time I stood at the counter alone. "Cheeseburger. Hold the pickle."

I'd decided to follow my gut, and my gut told me it was time to take care of business, time for the real Mona-lisa Kent to please stand up. Arm the nuclear warheads, I was making a preemptive strike.

I glanced back to see how many people were fast-fooding their breakfasts. Morning traffic was light. Only half of the tables were full, and no one waited behind the PLEASE WAIT TO BE SEATED—THANK YOU!!! sign. The Sunday brunch crowd probably hadn't rolled out of bed yet. Some grandmas a few tables to my left poked listlessly at their pancakes, but Frizzbeard's booth was empty, so no need to worry about his ancient eyes staring at me like *"Aha! I knew I knew you. You're That Monalisa Kent Girl!"*

Thing is, this time *everybody* was staring at me.

Maybe purple wasn't a big enough change. I'd dyed my hair violet late last night, thinking it would be a whole new disguise. People in this town weren't too sharp—or at least that's what I'd thought. But judging by the stares I got now, they were able to figure out that the blue-haired girl in the interview and the purple-haired girl in front of them were one and the same. So instead of buying myself a few minutes, I was spotted as soon as I walked in. It's like they were waiting for something interesting enough to make them actually focus their eyes.

Stay calm, Mona, stay calm, I chanted in my head. I picked a focal point, breathing slowly in and out while staring at the portraits hanging below the breakfast menu: three flattopped heads, three toothy smiles, three slicked handlebar mustaches—Muessa Junction's previous mayors, all former shift managers. They represented the pitiful history of Muessa Junction, a town that rose from the ashes on the backs of trust-fund students who craved university degrees and cheap, convenient meals away from home—two needs this fire-crippled town had scrambled desperately to satisfy. The fast-food industry was as much a part of the new Muessa Junction as my dad's "big ol' school down the street."

As usual, focusing on the past did nothing for me. My nerves still jangled. So I concentrated on blocking out the stares drilling into my back. It almost hurt, those eyes boring into me like heat rays. Darn spotlight again. Only this time, it felt more like one of those searchlights that rip through the night after a prison break. I was the escaping prisoner, all lit up, my getaway foiled. Torture would surely follow. I considered turning around and leaving, then and there.

I stayed.

Everyone was focused on me, as if waiting. Yet I hesitated. Should I really do this? It would shake up everything. No more hiding. No more backing down. No more feeling like a spineless loser.

The customers continued staring.

Maybe a dyed head wasn't what I needed. Maybe what I needed was a hat—a charred flour yarmulke, perhaps. . . .

In one sudden motion, I clamped my hand on top of my head, took a deep breath, then mounted the nearest table. My beat-up work boots thudded the molded plastic tabletop like gunshots. Not that I needed to get anyone's attention. I'd had that as soon as I clomp-stomped into the place with my blue—no, make that purple—hair. Heck, I'd had their attention since I was six.

My voice was shaky but loud. "Here's a thought—"

"Oh no, not you again." I heard the manager before I saw him. A bloodred warning flag unfurled in my brain. But I wasn't going to abort my mission.

I can do this. Just taking care of business.

I started again, this time loud and strong. "Well-behaved women seldom make history."

The customers looked bewildered.

Stick with it, Mona.

"Control your destiny, or someone else will."

Heads tilted and eyes squinted. The manager lurched around the counter. "Get down!"

But I didn't. "I'm not nearly as think as you confused I am."

Some smiles flashed. Aha! I knew they'd like that one. It always made *me* smile. Encouraged, I strung together two of my favorite bumper stickers, chanting them kind of singsongy, clapping my hands and stomping in tempo:

"Believe in those who seek the truth, doubt all those who find it. Open minds mean open hearts, to hell with those who mind it!"

The grandmas to my left whooped loudly and clapped along—"You tell 'em, dearie! Ethel, turn on your hearing aid. You don't want to miss this!" They clapped off-beat, but that didn't matter. I'd won them over. They weren't dead after all. Maybe this town still had some life in it yet.

The manager wasn't clapping, though. Scarlet splotches mottled his cheeky face, and the greasy tips of his graying handlebar mustache vibrated. An overpunctuated button pinned to his red, white, and yellow pinstriped shirt proclaimed Ask Me! I *LIKE* to help!!!

My mental red flag was vibrating as rapidly as the man's mustache. Time for me to skedaddle. Mr. Manager was obviously more than willing to assist me—just ask him, he'd *LIKE* to help!!!

I dropped to the floor, keeping the table between me and the burger dealer. His name badge was at eye level: OSWALD BEAN—BREAKFAST SHIFT MANAGER.

Stopping to read his badge was a mistake, though—I'd always been a slow reader. It gave Oswald Bean time to make his move. He lunged to his right as if to zip around the table and grab me. It was a pretty optimistic move, given his clear lack of athleticism. I dodged easily to my right. Then he lunged left, so I dodged left. We played Tag around the table, and I was It.

And, for a change, being It wasn't so bad.

I hollered as I juked side to side, "Those who dance are thought mad by those who hear not the music!"

The grannies pumped their fists in the air and barked. People at the tables near them laughed and started clapping, too.

"Stand up and march to your own drummer!"

Most people were cheering by then—"Hear, hear!" and "Darn tootin'!" and "Finally a little spunk in this town, eh, Ethel?"—and calling out to Oswald Bean to "Let her alone. She's not hurting anyone!"

Finally I master-juked the tubby man by feigning left, then breaking right, scuttling through the double doors so fast my shoes sounded like machine guns. *Clomp, clomp, clomp, clomp, clomp—Bang!* The doors slammed closed behind me.

Freedom! I had escaped. No more searchlights. No more torture. I was in control now. My fate was my own.

I twisted and fired one last salvo through the glass. "DIFFERENT DRUMMER? I'M MY OWN BAND!"

7

Back when I went to Muessa Junction Elementary, I loved watching Olympic gymnasts on TV. Itty-bitty girls with supersize muscles, flipping and flying through the air with the greatest of ease. They'd trained their whole thirteen-year lives for those few moments of competition. One event. One judging. One gold medal. My pulse fluttered as I imagined their excitement and passion, their fear and nervousness, their ultimate elation or crushing heartbreak. A life defined by a single performance. The concept fascinated me.

Now I'd gone and executed my own triple backflip to nail the gold. And I was still soaring. I'd given this town a little jolt, and its eyelids had fluttered. Maybe I'd been too quick to call its time of death.

I couldn't wait to share my victory with Binny. Boarding to his shop was like surfing on clouds. He'd be so proud. After all, he was the one who'd told me to stand up for myself, to take care of—

Huh? I skidded my board to a stop. Ahead of me Binny was in front of his shop, out on the sizzling sidewalk, roosting on his pillow like a fried egg on a griddle. I almost glanced skyward, half expecting two English muffins and a sausage patty to drop from the heavens and complete the scene.

I hadn't seen Binny *outside* his shop in at least, what, seven or eight years? Back when I was in fourth grade, probably, in the days when he stocked just one kind of bumper sticker, selling it out of a plywood booth patchworked together with duct tape and thumbtacks. People used to stroll up to the booth with thirst in their eyes, assuming it was a lemonade stand. God, I hate it when people assume. *Ass* of *u* and *me*, every time. A Muessa Junction specialty. Junctioners have done that to me for ten years, assumed they knew who I was because they knew what I did. At least Binny had the last laugh on them for assuming they knew what he was doing out there in a shack. They'd say, "How much for a large?" and he'd say, "Two bucks," and hand them a sticker: **Back the Boot— Support your local fire department.**

After Binny bought the building across from the plant

and expanded his sticker business, I never saw him outside again. Never. He slept in his shop instead of at home. Come to think of it, I didn't know if Binny even had a home. How he got food was beyond me, too. I never thought to ask. Just assumed that somehow he got food and ate it.

Uh-oh, *Mona* = ass.

My high-flying mood crashed hard. "Binny, what's wrong? How come you're out here on the sidewalk?"

He just sat there, Buddha-stiff as usual. He didn't respond. Not usual.

"Binny? What's up?"

A fly settled on his nose. Still he didn't move. His eyes remained fixed on a spot beyond my shoulder, as if he were watching a geyser, waiting for it to blow, refusing to blink and risk missing the spout.

Binny had never ignored me before. He'd ignored Glenn plenty of times, sure, but me? Never. I wasn't sure if I was more concerned or irritated.

Large splotches of sunlight bounced off of his head. Clearly the tattered BINFORD'S BUMPER STICKERS awning above him was useless, and the three spit-slicked hairs on his otherwise bald scalp were no protection. Even Binny— a forty-year resident of this sauna town and a former firefighter—would surely be broiled by extended exposure to Muessa Junction's merciless sun.

Concern won out. I had to do something. Before I could decide on an actual course of action, though, Binny spoke up. His grizzled voice sounded weak in the stale, fry-fumed air.

"Did you hear them sirens, Buttercup?"

"When? Just now? I didn't hear any sirens." I twisted and turned, looking for something that would shield him from the sun. "I heard sirens yesterday. Is that what you mean?"

"Yes, yes, the sirens." There, a hint of the old Binny, nice and snippy. Yet he still didn't move. "Who needs sirens? I smelled it." His nose wrinkled in disgust— movement!—startling the fly. Then he whispered, "I *still* smell it."

Not likely. Yesterday's fire was all the way across town. I'd seen the fire truck zoom that way with my own eyes, and later I'd heard Potter's report of how our hyper-paranoid firefighters used four massive hoses to douse one itty-bitty fryer of neglected onion rings. No big deal. Certainly no smoky inferno. Binny couldn't possibly smell the smoke that far away and a day later. And so what if he did?

"I smell smoke," he whispered once more. "I always smell it. Never this strong, though, not since . . . that night."

I grimaced at his reference to my infamous blaze. I'd messed up big-time, I knew that. I just wished people would forget about it. Especially me. But because burning down the plant almost put the whole town on welfare, the flames would probably burn in Junctioners' memories forever. Heck, they were so paranoid about fire that they'd call 911 if they saw a lit cigarette butt in the gutter. But could I blame them for not wanting to go down in flames a second time? My dad and the fast-food chains had resurrected them once. Who would do it the next time?

In a sudden burst of energy, Binny threw his quiver off his back, spilling incense rods all over the sidewalk, where they rolled among littered straw wrappers. "Incense, bah! Jasmine won't cover this smell anymore. Not now, not never." He glared at nothing. "Thirty years I fought it. Standin' up to it, thinkin' I could win. Fool!" He spit on the ground, just missing his right knee. "It won."

"Binny, what are you talking about?" I nearly begged the words, totally frustrated. "What won, the smoke? How can smoke win?"

Binny shook his fist at the air. "No, no, not the smoke! The *fire*. The fire won. Smoke is just the fire's voice, get me? Its voice!" A finger popped free of his fist and he wagged it, chastising the air. "People assume flames do the talking, but never assume things, never!"

Yeah, yeah—u, me, ass. I already knew that.

"*I* know better," he swore. "Flames are the tongues of the beast, lickin' at flesh—but tongues don't talk!" His voice became an intense whisper. "The smoke sliding off them tongues, that's what slips inside a body, fills the lungs, saturates the cells . . . communes with the soul." He dragged out the last word—"sooooooooul"—then broke off. His hand fell limp to his lap, his shoulders sagged, his burst of energy was spent. "Smoke an' flames an' heat—the trinity of fire. When it calls out, people tremble. But not me—no, not Binford Petit. Young and cocky, I was. I was invincible. I inhaled smoke and snorted it right back out, mocking it. I never trembled. Not until . . ."—he trailed off, then sighed heavily—"not until that damned-to-hell plant."

At the mention of the plant, I was forced to acknowledge the charred building behind me. I didn't look at it though. I never did, which wasn't easy. Smack dab in the center of town, that huge, burnt-out corpse was visible from every square foot of Muessa Junction. Rumor had it people had filled the place with old furniture over the years, used it as a hangout, a drug den, a lovers hideaway. Some even claimed it was haunted, telling of ghostly groans that oozed out of the holey rafters when the night sky was darkest. I wanted nothing to do with the place.

Exhausted and frustrated at once, I let my own shoulders sag and lolled my head back, trying to stretch out the tension. Though the scorching sun made me squint, my eyes came to rest on the sticker, now badly faded, that Binny had proudly stuck above his door at the shop's grand opening: Be the change you wish to see in the world.

I had to try once more. "Come on, Binny, let's go inside the shop."

"Inside!" I almost stumbled back from the force of his yell. His temper had more lives than Catwoman. "I should have gone inside the plant that night. I should have saved you. I *would* have saved you. . . . But no, I was a fool. Blinded by arrogance! That's why I didn't sense it when I faced it down, laughing my mighty laugh. That fire was waiting for me, Buttercup. When I inhaled, the smoke stormed my lungs, choking me. Then it lassoed my soul, yanked it right out of my body. I felt it! The shock. The emptiness. Then the fear flooding into the void . . . fear for myself. Myself! Two helpless babes needing rescue, and I protected my own sorry self! I turned tail, Buttercup. I cowered like a sewer rat. I convinced myself no one could cross those flames, that it was impossible. Impossible!" He shook his head. "But it wasn't impossible. Your papa crossed those flames when he toted you out. Your papa beat that fire. I lost. You were saved; Paco was saved; I was lost."

"Binny, this is crazy talk. Let's just go inside, okay?"

He didn't hear me. He was shivering, almost crying. "I lost my soul in that fire, Buttercup. It was stolen from me. I hear it calling, louder now than ever, my soul . . . the smoke . . . I smell it. . . ."

"Binny, look at me! You're not even looking at me." I racked my memory for a bumper sticker saying that would make this better. But I couldn't think of a single one.

Then I did it. The unthinkable. I turned and faced the plant, dead-on. I had to see what Binny was seeing.

The huge, broken building looked unstable at best: crumbled, holey walls, cracked slab floors, charred wooden posts, blackened cement columns that barely supported the bits of sagging roof that remained. . . . The Wayne family had designed it to resemble their sprawling family castle back in the old country, but they'd cut corners in the building of it. They'd filled the inside of the three-story castle with cheap pine and flaky stucco, and instead of using sturdy stone for the walls, they used pebbly cement. Three of the four rounded parapets still stood high, but the fourth one was just a pile of charred rubble, like most of the rest of the former castle. The full scope of the W. family stinginess came out after the fire. The cost of rebuilding it the safe way was probably one of the reasons they didn't rebuild. They'd meant their three-story fortress to house a factory and to make money, not to last forever. But last it did—even a four-alarm fire hadn't razed it.

Glenn had tried a few times to get me to go inside the burnt plant, but no way. Not me. Now, as I looked upon it directly for the first time in a decade, my pulse fluttered in fear and nervousness and anger. My whole sixteen-year life revolved around that building. One night. One misjudgment. One fire. A life defined by a single experience. The concept nauseated me.

My stomach executed a triple flip and landed with a thud.

A pair of gloomy, glassless windows on a corner wall leveled a vacant stare my way. I turned my back on them and looked down at Binny. I'd never suspected he felt like a failure about that night. *I* had always felt like the failure, the loser, the one who ruined everything. Binny was the famous firefighter, the hero.

The Earth had indeed turned on its head, I was sure of that now. My world had become a place where heroes were failures and failures were heroes.

It was my turn to shiver.

8

What you see is not what you get. If I'd learned nothing else in the day and a half since Selina's interview, I'd learned that. Binny the failed hero, my dad the heroic failure, me the . . . well, I was beginning to suspect that everyone had somebody else inside them, hidden from judging eyes. Maybe that's why superheroes are so popular. Movies, comics, cartoons . . . people can't get enough of caped crusaders. The idea that inside geeks, wimps, and losers lurks someone special and undefeatable is pretty darn attractive—especially to geeks, wimps, and losers. Heck, I wouldn't mind waking up one day to see Wonder

Woman in my mirror. That babe deflects bullets with her bracelets; think what she'd do to evil stares.

With my life, though, the character showing up in my mirror would probably be the crazy Mad Hatter.

I'd left Binny sitting on the sidewalk. What else could I do? On the chance that Glenn would have one of his brilliant ideas about him, I skated over to Dante's. But when I reported Binny's sidewalk sitting and his feeling like a failure that night, Glenn just positioned his Batman bill between me and his glasses—like if he didn't see me, I wasn't there.

Apparently I'd interrupted a tutoring session. *Excuse me, fellas.* Glenn was painstakingly teaching Burt the proper way to wield a tattoo needle. The victim of their efforts was a mangled, dripping grapefruit. In Burt's small hand, the yellowish ball looked more basketball than fruit, and the vibrating needle stuttered and gouged like a jackhammer gone berserk. They seemed to think it was pretty funny, laughing each time the needle skidded and sent juice squirting. I wouldn't want to be any closer to Burt and that needle than I was at that moment. But the kid hung on gamely, mumbling "hugger-mugger" over and over. It must have been his new word of the day. He, too, had on a hat, so now both boys could make shields of their bills—Glenn with his sacred Batman, Burt with a spanking new Robin, Boy Wonder.

Could the Mad Hatter kick Batman's butt? I gave that

question some serious thought as I stood there, ignored and clenching my fists.

It was into this tense environment that Roy stumbled, lugging a can of paint. For all his huffing and puffing, I expected a whole keg of paint to be weighing down his long arm, not just that gallon can. As usual, he was wearing his black T-shirt with the big, yellow smiley face. The graphic was so festive and round compared to the sharp angles of Roy's beaky face. He plunked the paint can on the floor with a bang, then stood straight, peered down at me, puckered up his lips, and whistled like a construction worker.

The whistle caught me off guard. I never would've pegged Roy as a whistler. And I was just wearing jeans and work boots, not anything to be whistling all macho-man over. I was about to unleash the Mad Hatter on him when he grinned and said, "Heard about your poetry raid this morning, Mona. I just saw Potter up the street, and he says everyone's talking about it. You'd think it was the Second Coming or something." He whistled again, like he was impressed. "I knew you weren't born to be a wallflower. It's not your nature."

"Poetry raid?"

"Word's spreading fast about your performance—*both* performances, actually. I guess people dig it. Go figure."

That got Glenn's attention. "What are you babbling about, Roy? Mona, what did you do now?"

"What, you're not ignoring me now?" I said.

"Like you'd ever let that happen."

"Mona," Burt interrupted me and Glenn, "you didn't stand on a table and yell again, did you? I wanted to do it with you next time." His mouth turned down in a pout, and his eyes got moist. For a second, I thought he was going to cry.

"It wasn't a big table," I said.

"Big or not," Roy said, "everyone is talking about it. Some say you're making trouble again, but the others are just glad to have something interesting to talk about for a change. It's invigorating. You sure know how to hog the limelight, Monalisa Kent."

Glenn snorted. "So much for lying low. Come on, Burt. I'll show you something *really* cool." He snatched Burt's massacred grapefruit and tossed it into the garbage, then half urged, half pushed the Boy Wonder out the door.

I tried to call them back, but they moved too quickly. As I watched Glenn's back disappear, I had the awful sensation of my heart being tugged and stretched behind him like a strand of taffy. At least Burt flashed me a quick smile as he was scuttled out.

What was Glenn's problem? More and more he was moody like that. Just like more and more he was AWOL when I showed up at Dante's to claim him. Used to be Glenn and I did nothing separately. Tuck used to call us the Wonder Twins—not that the two of us had ever worn matching ball caps.

117

"Roy, can I ask you something?"

"You just did."

I clenched my jaw hard, muzzling my snotty response. As I struggled to remain civil, his playful grin withered.

This was too important to get sidetracked, though, so I tried again. "I was just thinking . . . you spend a lot of time with Glenn, with your car art and all. Do you think he's acting kind of weird lately?"

He seemed about to say something. Then he paused. Then he asked, "Weird how?"

"I don't know. Weird like . . . well, like he doesn't like being around me anymore."

"Oh, Mona, I'm sure he likes being around you."

"Well, he doesn't act like it. Not lately, anyway."

He eyed me kind of sideways. "You're probably imagining it."

Probably *not*. As much as it pained me to admit it, lately—especially the last few days—whenever Glenn and I were together, Glenn acted like he didn't want to be. Like he had somewhere else he wanted to go and he was impatient to get there. And all his fidgeting and snorting and being sarcastic . . . well, he acted like I annoyed him. "No, I'm not imagining it. Something's wrong with him."

Roy eyed me again. "Maybe something's wrong with you."

"Me? What's wrong with me?"

He shrugged. "I'm just saying, people don't usually think they have anything to do with it when their world spins the wrong way. Maybe they should look at themselves first."

"I have enough people looking at me, thank you."

"Hey, you asked me."

He had me there. And he was right, I wasn't quite myself lately—dying my hair, jumping onto tables, hollering bumper-stickerisms in crowded restaurants. But yesterday was the eleventh. That threw me off every year; Glenn should've known that. Only, to be honest, now that I thought about it, I probably felt more "myself" after the Frizzbeard incident than I ever had. Which meant it had to be Glenn who had the problem, not me. Glenn just couldn't deal, that's all. He didn't understand what it was like to know you did something so incredibly stupid and hurt so many people. He didn't have to relive his blunder every year. Okay, he was in the fire, too, but that wasn't the same. He didn't set it. He didn't have to deal with what I had to deal with.

And anyway, whoever's fault it was, as each day passed, Glenn and I seemed to have less and less in common besides the fact that we'd been best friends since birth.

And now Glenn had Burt.

"Roy, do you have any friends you've known since you were little?"

He thought about that a moment. "No, not like you and Glenn. But then, I'm not like you, Mona. I know a lot of people a little bit; you know a few people well. It's hard to keep up a deep friendship when you're spread thin." He turned away to nudge and shove at the paint can with his foot, trying to get it under the futon. Between shoves, he muttered about ankle weights. Mission finally accomplished, he turned and looked down at me again. "But when I do, it sticks." He gazed at me a moment longer. "Did you ever meet my sister, Precioso?"

"Your sister's name is Precioso?"

"Yes. She was named after my grandma, on my mom's side."

"Your grandma's name was Precioso?"

"Yes. It's a common Filipino name, Mona."

"Filipino?" I scrutinized Roy's pale face. He looked nothing like the dark-haired, dark-skinned Filipino kids who peppered Muessa Junction's proudly multicultural citizenry. "Since when are you Filipino? How did I not know this?"

"Did you ever ask?"

Oh. I buttoned my lips.

"I take after my dad," he said. "He was a basketball player back in Sweden—*yes,* they play *basketball* in Sweden. My point is, Precioso is a lot like you. Hot tempered and prickly and always into something. Too bad you never met her—you two would get along great." I made a face but didn't interrupt him. "I miss having Preci around all the time. She's not like Judd." Roy's turn to make a face. "Judd's just plain mean."

I hadn't met Roy's older brother, either, but I knew Judd by sight and by reputation. "Mean" was an understatement. Taller and bulkier than Roy and hairy as a go-rilla, Judd was rumored to rip apart cars with his bare hands at the auto wrecking yard.

"Preci is eight years older than me, but she always looked out for me when I was growing up, kept Judd from power-tripping on me. She was around more than my folks were." He pulled a stuffed wallet from the front pocket of his clown jeans and dug out what must have been an old senior yearbook photo. Preci's face was skinny and pale like Roy's, but pretty. She had his easy smile and lashy eyes. "When she turned eighteen, she married her kindergarten sweetheart and moved over to Rancho Mesa. She comes back now and then to have Tuck tattoo her. Last time she was here, he inked portraits of her two sons on her shoulder, just above a heart that says TRUE LOVE. When she got home, her husband asked why she hadn't had his face tattooed there, too. Know what she told him?"

I shook my head.

"She told him she doesn't want him getting cocky. Tat-toos are permanent, and tattooing him onto her body would be like giving him a guarantee. She wants to keep him on his toes. They've been friends forever, and she wants them to stay that way. Preci says forever friendships are the first ones to wilt from neglect."

I didn't want to ask the question that came to mind, but I knew I had to: "You think that's what's happening with me and Glenn?"

121

He shrugged. "A dog will heel only as long as he wants to."

"Hey, I'm not making anybody heel."

He put his hands up and stepped back. "Like I said, you asked."

Okay, fine. Whatever the stupid reason, Glenn and I were drifting apart. What was I supposed to do about it? Glenn was always the fixer. Like that time he welded wings to my fifth-grade science fair project, turning my leaky submarine into a ribbon-winning jumbo jet. Or that day in eighth grade when he pulled the fire alarm to get me out of the math test I'd forgotten to study for—well, I hadn't really *forgotten*. Without that evacuation, I surely would've landed that F I'd dodged all semester. I could think of a million other times Glenn had covered my back and stepped up when a problem needed solving. He always fixed the problems.

Only this time, he *was* the problem.

I took a deep breath. Glenn and I *would* be friends forever. I'd make sure of it. No more neglect. I'd figure out what was broken and find a way to fix it. I could be a problem solver, too. And no one would have to *heel* in the process.

"I don't even know what Glenn likes to do these days," I admitted to Roy. "It seems like lately he just takes off."

"It's not like he goes very far."

"What do you mean?"

"He just goes over to the plant."

122

"The plant? No way!"

"Yes way. I see him duck in there all the time. He goes in through the old employee entrance. You could see it from the futon if you'd ever looked." He plopped down onto the futon and absently flapped a long, bony arm in the direction of the door. He opened an issue of *Flash Talk,* flipped to the one-color portraits section, and squeezed his blue racquetball with one hand while turning pages with the other.

I didn't know the entrance Roy was talking about. A main goal of my life had always been to ignore the charred castle. I certainly wouldn't sit on the futon and moon at it like it was the Grand Canyon or something. But now, for the second time in one day, I decided to confront that burnt-out nightmare for the sake of a friend.

Quickly, like yanking off a Band-Aid, I strode over to Roy and leaned in, lining my head up between him and the Dante's door. Just like Roy said, I had a clear view of the plant.

Roy was also right about the entrance. I could see it, right over the Plymouth Knight's left carburetor. There was no actual door, just a doorway, and that was questionable at best. I could tell it used to be rectangular, but now it was so crumbled and crisscrossed with burnt beams and fallen poles that I couldn't imagine anyone just "ducking" through it. The rounded parapet walls around the doorway seemed fairly complete, though—more so than any other part of the former factory, which seemed to sag threateningly where anything stood at all. I suppose I would have noticed that entranceway a long time ago if I'd ever given the plant more than the occasional accidental one-second glance.

Ugh. Looking at the ruins so long and straight on made me sweat, actually sweat.

By the time I reached the service entrance, I was drenched. Every footstep between Dante's and the plant had been hotter than the one before, and sticking my head through the partly crumbled doorway was like sticking my head in an oven. Up close I found it was possible to duck through after all, with the fallen beams and poles having left holes here and there that were big enough to squeeze into. I hesitated one last moment, then scooched through.

The hallway on the other side of the debris was less blocked. It was faintly lighted by dapples of sunlight that snuck in through the poles and beams, but that died out after a few feet. To see anything at all, I had to depend on the handful of determined rays that slipped in through charred, jagged holes in the walls and ceiling. In that dim haze, everything looked singed and sooty. The smell of smoke was distinct; the air seemed laced with ash. I could just make out a cleared footpath snaking through the debris-covered cement floor. It led down a narrow hallway that took a sharp right turn maybe twenty feet away. Stray wooden beams poked down from the ceiling every few feet, but nothing as extreme as what I'd crawled through in the doorway. I stooped and moved forward.

With each shuffling step, the smell of smoke got stronger. I wiped my runny nose and drippy forehead. That woozy feeling was back, and I'd have sworn on a hotel Bible that I heard vague sirens and yells and—

Was that a groan?

Shuddering, I made myself keep stoop-walking down a mazelike tunnel, following the footpath, twisting and turning at the mercy of the beams and crumbled stucco. The light grew dimmer.

Oh, this is a very very bad idea, Monalisa Kent.

Yet still I moved forward. Why? Curiosity? No way! Concern for Glenn? Maybe. . . . No, no I wouldn't say it was either of those, actually. My motive seemed less logical or thoughtful than that. More than anything, what propelled me forward was a feeling, a mix of dread and determination. It was the same feeling I experienced whenever I had to do something I didn't want to—like when I had to dig a splinter out of my own finger, knowing it would hurt like hell and not wanting to do it, but knowing I *would* do it because I couldn't leave the bloody thing in there, now could I?

So I continued onward, full of dread yet determined.

For balance, I reached out and ran my hands along a half-tumbled wall. It felt dusty and gritty. The texture was surprising, really, because I'd half expected to put my hand right through the wall, as might happen in a dream.

Then I heard noises to my right. Voices? I angled that way, eventually coming upon a pile of charred metal futon frames propped against the tunnel wall. I paused to examine a flickering orange glow on the cement floor, just visible at one corner of the pile. The glow seemed brighter near the base of the wall. I bent closer.

At that moment, faint wisps of smoke puffed through the skeletal ribbing of the futon, right into my face. I nearly bolted out, then and there. Smoke is never good. Just ask Binny.

But I had to see. I'd come too far to turn tail. Maybe I was being like Binny used to be, foolish and cocky. I paused a moment, thinking about that, only I couldn't picture myself sitting on the sidewalk ten years from now babbling about smoky futon skeletons. Maybe foolish and cocky would work for me. Holding my breath, I shoved the futon frames aside with unexpected ease. Behind was a gash in the wall, near the floor. It was about as wide as my shoulders and as high as my knees, and the floor there was clear of dust and debris.

I exhaled slowly, hesitating once more. Then, setting my jaw firmly, I dropped to my knees and crawled forward through the hole—and into another realm.

Or so the room beyond struck me. Wide and round and cavelike, it looked untouched by the fire that had ravaged the rest of the fortress a decade ago. I was probably in one of the rounded parapets. Except for a sunlit square on a distant wall—a high window?—the lighting came from several candelabras positioned around the room. All about me, shadows danced in rippling red-

126

yellow-orange spotlights. In the center of the circular room I saw Glenn and Burt.

Only, I didn't quite understand what I was witnessing. There was a lighter in Burt's hand. And in Glenn's hand was a large piece of paper, flames quickly devouring it.

"Glenn! What are you doing?"

Glenn jerked as though stung by a bee. The paper dropped to the floor. He stomped out the small flames with three quick taps of his large foot.

The expression on his face was too hard to read in the waxy light. It could have been anger. Or maybe guilt. Tough call. I knew the expression on my face, though: shock—complete, total shock. It was one thing to light candles, but igniting other stuff, well, Glenn only needed to look at the crumbled building around him to see how bad an idea that was. He should know better than anyone.

Not that Glenn was afraid of fire. I was the one who was afraid of it. I couldn't even be in the general vicinity when he and Roy welded their car art.

"What are you trying to do, burn the place down?" Stupid comment, but I said it anyway.

"Mona? What are you doing in here?" Glenn said. "You never come in here."

"I never play with fire, either."

Burt piped up in defense of his idol. "We weren't playing, Mona. Glenn was just showing me his gallery. Cool, huh?"

"His gallery?"

"Yeah, look." Burt reflicked his lighter, sending a miniature flame shooting upward. He held it up to a curved wall. Dim outlines of old futons came into focus in the light of his tiny torch. He climbed onto one of them to get closer to the wall he was spotlighting.

I inched closer, too. The wall was covered with drawings and paintings. They were scratched, penciled, and inked directly onto the pebbly cement like hieroglyphics. A lot were tribal designs like Chet's eye tattoo, but even more were colorful paintings of comic book heroes with capes and bulging muscles and lasers shooting from superhuman eyeballs.

Then Burt lit up a stretch of wall that was more mural-like, a full-color painting with rolling green hills, stormy skies, and a metropolis in flames. In the center was a skyscraper with a dark-haired damsel in distress. I struggled to make out the figures at the far right, just beyond the lighter's range. It looked like Batman doing battle with a fire-tongued dragon. Or maybe that was Godzilla.

"You did this, Glenn?" I asked.

"I love this room," he said, like that answered my question. "But it needed pizzazz."

He took the lighter back from Burt, who was grinning at him, and snapped it closed.

I tried to process what I was seeing: the mural and scratchings on the cavelike walls, the half-burned drawing—what was that, another fire-breathing Godzilla?—the candelabras. It was all so dreamlike—or maybe nightmarelike.

At least the candles kept bloodsucking bats at bay; the corners probably teemed with them.

Obviously Glenn spent a lot of time here. This place must be important to him. That wasn't bad, was it? I mean, even Batman had his Batcave. But why did it have to be such a big secret? From me, no less. He'd known Burt only a few days, yet he'd told Burt.

"Mona." Burt's voice came from behind me now. "Did you know Glenn could draw so good? I wish I could draw that good. Glenn can draw anything."

Well, of course he could. He's Glenn. Whatever he did, he did well. Got a munched-up car? Glenn will turn it into a dining room table. Got a leaky submarine? Glenn will turn it into an airplane. Got a wad of chewing gum? Glenn will turn it into a musical instrument. Glenn's talents went without saying—which was a good thing, because I couldn't say anything. I was reeling from surprise—and hurt. My thinking was further clouded by the candle smoke, which sent my tummy wooziness up to my brain. The flickers and dancing shadows were Twinkie City. My ears were ringing with the distant, ghostly sound of sirens—

Sirens! Stop the sirens!

No! No flashback! Not now. I rubbed my temples and tried to focus. That's when I saw him—Daddy. Only he wasn't there, not really; it was just a flashback, a memory finally jogged loose. Young and not so life worn, the image of Daddy floated just behind Glenn, barely visible in the weak candlelight. He wasn't looking at me with his sad eyes, though. He wasn't looking at any of us. He was gazing at something in his hand. A long metal tool. He might've even been crying. His free hand rose to the tool and flicked a switch; then flames erupted from the steel tube. I gasped as Glenn swooped his arm up to point to the wall, extending it right through my imaginary dad and the flames. I knew they weren't there, that this was a flashback, but they seemed so real.

I ducked my head and covered my eyes, blotting out the smoke or the vision; I didn't know which. Not that it mattered—my lids were closed, but the resurfacing memory didn't need my eyes. All this flashback needed was my mind. And in my mind I saw a close-up of the welding torch dropping at Glenn's feet, igniting the futon batting piled next to him. Of Daddy dropping it. Of Daddy starting the fire. It was my memory, and it was real.

I turned and ran. Barely seeing, barely thinking, I dove for the gash in the wall and scrambled through it. I got up and ran through the hallway, stooping and running, fast but not fast enough, not fast enough. . . . I could hear the sirens again, and the yelling, the screaming . . . my screaming. . . . "Daddy, Daddy! Where are you, Daddy? I can't see you! Daddy!"

9

Freaking out like a basket case was not my usual behavior—not before this weekend, anyway. But then, it wasn't usual to discover that my dad had thrown me to the wolves to cover his own rear end. My dad had started that plant fire, and then he had blamed it all on me, his own daughter.

No wonder I could never remember setting the fire. I *didn't* set it.

The flashback of my dad had seared me to the core, and when I ran, it was as though I was trying to put out flames all over my body. I succeeded only in fanning them. Glenn and Burt had chased after me, hollering at me to stop and come back. But I ran on. With Glenn's clumsy slowness and Burt's hummingbird legs, they gave up by the first corner.

Now here I was, tearing through my house, screaming "Dad!" at the top of my lungs. Only this time, anger fueled my screams, not fear.

But my dad was nowhere in the house. He was probably taking his postinterview stroll, waving and smiling and patting people on the back like a benevolent king gracing his subjects with his royal presence.

The traitor.

I ended up in my room, breathing hard, looking about wildly. For what?

HONK IF YOU LIKE HORNS.

Something to calm me, maybe.

Be reasonable. Do it MY way.

Words of wisdom to make things all right.

KEEP THE BOOKS. BURN THE CENSORS.

Only there was nothing there to calm me.

I brake for . . . wait . . . AAAH! NO BRAKES!

A thousand bumper stickers plastered those walls, yet not one of them covered backstabbing dads. Stupid stickers—here I'd collected them forever, but when I really needed them, *nada*. They were no use at all. Now what was I supposed to do? I felt paralyzed and frantic at once. *Someone tell me what to do!* Then I knew.

❖ ❖ ❖

"*Bebita*, how do you know it was *tu papá*?"

When I'd exploded into the Pink Cloud, I'd ripped back a frilly curtain to reveal Margarita etching a heart—of course—onto some blond girl's hip. The instant Margarita laid eyes on my freaked-out face, she stood up and called out to Talula to come and take over her needle.

Now we were both in the Hole and Margarita was wearing that wannabe-mom expression that usually creeped me out. Only at this most awful moment in the history of the universe, it did not.

"*Bebita, tu papá*, he loves you. He would not do what you say."

"I'm telling you, Margarita. I saw him. I saw him with the blowtorch. I saw it drop. I remember it all now. I'm not lying!"

"No, no, I do not say you lie. You are Mona, and Mona does not lie. It is just . . . *ay-ay-ay, Bebita, tu papá* is so sad, *sí,* but he is not so cruel."

She was pacing as much as a person could pace in the Hole, in itty-bitty half steps. A hint of lilies scented the air. I was propped against a wall, afraid to move, afraid of bumping into the mini stove or something else burning hot and full of sting.

I was full of sting myself. "All these years, he made me believe I did it. The whole town thinks it was me. But it wasn't me. It was him. Why would he do that?"

Margarita stopped her pacing and slumped down to the floor. My own legs started to sag. It was all too much.

With her face in her hands, Margarita sighed. "*Bebita, tu papá* is a good man. At least, he was. When *tu mamá* married him, she was so happy. He loved her like I never saw before, not in real life. They were so happy when they learned you were coming to them, a miracle of their love. All the world was right. A wee *bebita* for them both to love hard. But I worried, *Bebita*. I always worried. Loving hard, it is dangerous."

On the floor beside her now, I felt my face squinching like Burt's, which almost made me laugh. I choked back a dry heave instead.

This time, when Margarita reached over and put her hand on my back, I didn't stiffen.

"Losing *tu mamá*, it was the end of the world for him, I know this. He loves you, *Bebita*. He does. But that day his heart, it turned as hard as his love. Hard with pain. Or maybe he made his heart hard to keep out pain; this I do not know. But what I do know is, he is not evil, *Bebita*. He is just sad, so sad. Many times I try to help, for him, for *tu mamá,* for you most of all. But there is no helping a man who will not be helped."

My head and stomach and heart roiled with conflicting emotions. How come I'm not enough for him? He's always been enough for me. Even with all his sitting and staring at walls I've always loved him. "I hate him. I *hate* him!"

"*Ay, Bebita,* no. *Tu papá,* he is a musty onion, that is all." Margarita rubbed my back soothingly. "One cannot

134

hate the onion. It is the sass of the salsa, the soul of the soup. One must cut off the mold, inside is the good. All cooks, this they know." She sighed once more. "But *tu papá,* he fears the knife. To cut away his mold is to cut away his beloved. For him, this is to lose her, and this he cannot do. *Ay, Bebita,* it is not you, you do no wrong. It is *tu papá.* He stews in memories of the love lost to him." She shook her head slowly, sadly. "Memory can be beautiful, but it can be cruel, too. *Tu papá,* he remembers only the death. He forgets the life. *Tu mamita,* she was so full of life—like you."

I thought about the woman my dad mourned so deeply. I felt no connection to her; I never had. It was enough dealing every day with a father who was slipping away from me. Who had time for a mom I never met? My dad never said much about anything, let alone about her, but I'd heard all the stories about the old days from the Glenns, the days when my dad and my mom were young and wild, doing crazy stunts with Margarita and Tuck. They were all real artsy, like most Junctioners back then— Tuck and Mom with their painting, my dad with his number-one ranking on the national furniture design circuit, and Margarita with her creative schemings to turn their art into money. It was Margarita's idea to start the tattoo parlors. My dad was the only one who stayed out of the inking business. Instead he retired from the travel-heavy competition circuit and freelanced his revolutionary futon designs to Wayne Furniture. But then I replaced my mom—even taking her name—and my dad's genius withered. No creativity, no new designs, no money. Eventually he signed on as Wayne's futon frame manager, a mindless administrative job.

Even as a little girl, I knew my dad was just going through the motions. He'd get sparks now and then—designing the occasional futon, welding the occasional frame—but mostly he just punched his time card, at work and at home. That was why I spent more and more time with the Glenns. Babysitting me turned into a full-time gig for them after the fire, because after that blazing night, even the motions were too much for my dad.

Now I finally knew why.

Life can go from zero to sixty in a heartbeat. Two short days ago I knew who I could count on, I knew where I belonged, and—though at the time it seemed unbearable—my worst problem was staring strangers. Then July eleventh hit, and everything went upside down. Glenn had a groupie. Binny lived on the sidewalk, mumbling about souls and smoke. And my dad had No Vacancy tattooed on his heart to compliment the Vacancy sign on his forehead.

I was never one to sit around and mope—like father, *not* like daughter—so even though I had nowhere to go, I stepped onto my board and let the wheels simply roll, heading no place in particular, having no thoughts in particular. Every once in a while I poked a booted toe down and pushed, but mostly I just stood on the wood, shoulders drooped low, arms dangling, wheels rotating slowly. I considered rolling Binny's way, but as I barely had energy for my own traumas, I didn't really see a point in trying to buck him up right then. And Glenn, well, why would he want me around? He's got Burt and his super-secret Batcave now.

The streets were dotted with walkers and window-shoppers, their shorts and sunglasses the only concessions to the waves of heat lapping against the storefronts. Occasional wisps of warm air stirred the wrappers that littered the street. As usual, people were looking and pointing at me, but this time something was different. This time they were smiling, not scowling. The hostility was gone. I processed this observation much like a person sleep-walking.

Not even caring where I was, I rolled past the spot where the Wienerschnitzel delivery guy gave me such a hard time for ruining his life. There was no sign of him to-day. Up ahead a thick, gnarled branch on the climbing tree in front of Burger King hung low, catching my attention, tempting me to swing up and sit for a while. But I just didn't have the energy to swing up anywhere. Glenn and I used to sit on that branch for hours at a time when we were little, disappearing into the leaves where no one could see us, watching cars funnel through the drive-thru while we shared French fries and chicken nuggets. Over and over the cars stopped in front of the giant menu board and hollered into the speaker, "I want a Whopper! A large French fry! An apple pie! And a large Sprite! . . . What? . . . No, I said Sprite! . . . Sprite! . . . Large! . . . What? . . . No, apple! . . . Thank you!" We heard so many orders that eventually we could guess what the order would be just by looking at the make and condition of the cars. Like that beater pickup that just drove up with the MJHS Wrestling flag. It'll be a plain hamburger, definitely. Probably two. And a Coke. Most pickups were big on meat and straight cola, cut the frills.

I stopped and listened to see if I was right.

"I want a hamburger! No onions! No ketchup! No mustard!" *Bingo.* "And put some pineapple on that!" Pineapple? What kind of crackpot ordered pineapple on a hamburger at a Burger King drive-thru? "Yes, pineapple! . . . But that's what I want! You're supposed to do it my way! . . . Doesn't matter, that's my way! . . . Because the customer's always right! . . . I am *not* disturbing the peace, I'm disturbing the comfortable! . . . Oh, yeah? Maybe I *will* make my own!" The truck peeled out and zipped right past the flattopped boy peering out the little square window at the far end of the drive-thru.

When the dust cleared, I dropped the hand that covered my mouth and nose and pushed my board rolling again. *People are freaks.*

But at least that freak knew a good bumper sticker saying when he saw it. That was the same line I'd used

138

yesterday morning. For years I'd been trying to *disguise* or *distract,* but it was *disturb* that finally felt right. Maybe that pickup truck would discover the same thing. More people should think about disturbing the comfortable.

Being on the downward slope of a very slight hill, I didn't have to push anymore, since I didn't care that I was going about as fast as a snail. I just let my body go slack and my mind zone out until I came to the intersection and had to stop or be run over. I pressed the button for the crossing signal. To my right, about ten feet away, a kid with a flattop, sunglasses, and headphones was spinning a big, red, rectangular plastic sign in front of him, throwing it up into the air and catching it over and over, all the while dancing in place to his personal music box. In hand-scrawled white paint the sign read 3 BURGERS FOR A BUCK! THIS WAY ➡.

I couldn't stand it. I had to ask. "What are you doing?"

He just kept dancing and spinning his sign. I leaned sideways, into his line of vision, and waved my hand. "What are you doing?"

"What?" he said, letting go of the sign with one hand and lifting his headphones off of one ear.

"What are you doing?"

"I'm sign twirling. Three burgers for a buck, that way. Deal of the century." He pointed to the empty field behind him on the southwest side of the intersection. Only it wasn't empty now. Half of it was filled with parked cars.

The other half had a big, smoky barbeque fired up on it, with a flattopped boy in a blue polo shirt flipping burgers on the grill. Three more flattopped boys in blue polo shirts rushed around him, grabbing hamburgers from the grill and buns from packages stacked next to it. They'd plop a burger in a bun, squirt ketchup onto it, wrap it in newspaper, then hand it to one of the customers lined up behind a card table, who then shuffled to another table a few feet away. That table had a cooler on it with a sign that read FREE SODA. WE ♥ OUR CUSTOMERS!!! A tarp was strung up between some old telephone poles and the lone tree, and blankets lined the shaded ground. People ate their burgers picnic style, laughing and batting around a beach ball that had BILLY'S BURGERS written on it in big black marking pen letters.

"What's all that?" I asked the sign twirler.

"Only the next biggest burger chain in the world," he said proudly. The sun was behind my back, so he had to squint to look at me.

"Are you Billy?"

He nodded.

Talk about freaks. In any given direction, there was a Burger King, a McDonald's, and a Wendy's a half a block away. What was Billy thinking? Sweat was pouring down his face, and his blue polo shirt was dark with sweat around his neck and under his arms. I thought of Binny out in this heat, slow roasting on the sidewalk.

"You're crazy standing out here waving that sign," I

said. "Why don't you just lean it against the streetlight post and go sit in the shade?"

"Can't. People only notice signs if they move."

I raised my eyebrows. "Says who?"

"Says me. It made *you* stop."

He had a point. I looked at the big, happy picnic under the tarp. "You stopped a lot of other people, too." I gave him a mental A+ for creativity—something on short supply in Muessa Junction.

"Told you. And the burgers are the best. Better than Burger King." He tapped the tiny logo above his heart.

I was confused. "You work for Burger King?"

"I did." He spit into the gutter. "For two years, doing everything they asked. But this morning when I asked for a raise, you know what the manager said? He said no way, a monkey could do what I do. Well, can a monkey do this?" He flung the plastic sign up over his head, spun a three-sixty, then lifted his leg up and reached under, catching the sign in his hand.

I couldn't help it, I clapped.

He pointed to his impromptu restaurant and the guys manning the grill and table. They must have abandoned the Burger King with him. "See? It's packed. Billy's Burgers is going to kick Burger King's butt." He flipped his middle finger in the direction of Burger King and hollered at the lone car in the parking lot, "I'm controlling my *own* destiny now!" He squinted my way again. "Hey, don't I know you? I do! You're That Monalisa Kent G—"

141

"No, I'm not." The red hand in the crossing sign switched to a white WALK, and I pushed off fast. Billy shouted something behind me, but I couldn't hear it over the sound of the eighteen-wheeler McDonald's delivery truck that roared through the intersection between us.

Safely on the other side of the intersection, I looked back over my shoulder once more. Billy was back at his sign twirling again, and the eighteen-wheeler was turning into Billy's makeshift parking lot. The kid had stopped yet another customer. Maybe he was right—Billy's Burgers just might be the next biggest burger chain in the world.

Up ahead I saw the street sign for Togo Avenue. That was a far quieter street than this one, more residential. At the corner I leaned hard right, turning onto Togo. There I thought I could roll around in peace for a while.

I was wrong.

About half a block ahead of me, an Oompa Loompa, leashed to a wild boar, crossed to my side of the street. *Either this town is flipping out, or I am.* Bearing down on me quickly, the creatures soon revealed themselves to be, in reality, a fat man and his scroungy dog. The man's hand was locked in a death grip on the taut leash, and while he strained backward, he pressed his free hand against his straining shoulder as if to hold it in its socket.

I gasped. It was Oswald Bean, Breakfast Shift Manager.

He's gonna sic his dog on me! In the split second it took me to perk up and whip my head around in search of an escape route, Oswald Bean hollered out, "Yoo-hoo!"

142

Not "Sic her!" Not "Kill her!" Not "Rip her throat out, demon dog from Hell!"

Yoo-hoo.

It was just unexpected enough to confuse my muddled mind, which stuttered my toe push, which gave Oswald Bean a full nanosecond of opportunity, which he seized by following yoo-hoo with "Ms. Kent! Ms. Kent! I'm so glad I saw you."

Glad he saw me? Yesterday he would've been glad he killed me. My bewilderment was paralyzing.

"Ms. Kent," Oswald Bean huffed out when he reached me. His handlebar mustache vibrated with each puff. "Customers have been asking about you all morning. They want to know when your next performance is. I'm so sorry, Ms. Kent. I didn't know you were performing. I've never seen performance art before. I've heard about it— mimes, trolley dancing, that sort of thing. But I've never seen it. I'm so sorry. Will you please come back?"

Clearly God was having a laugh fest at my expense. I'd figured Roy was spouting off with fancy art words when he'd said people were talking about those "performances," or that Potter had just been putting Roy on when he told Roy that his customers were talking about my performances during his meat route. But then two separate people quoted my quotes and a guy who'd wanted to dunk my head in the fryer yesterday was yoo-hooing and asking me to come back and holler from his tabletops again. This was crazy.

Oswald Bean's knee-high dog betrayed no softness of heart, however. The brute's hard, trembling muscles and guttural whine terrified me. I could feel a trembling of my own, down in my pushing toe, which was trying to recruit the rest of my toes in one desperate, united push-off.

Luckily my brain won the battle with my revolting toes. Clenching my tootsies firmly, I locked my entire body statue still. That's what you're supposed to do if a bear scares you: stand still. Or better yet, play dead. No wait, maybe you're supposed to wave your arms and scream? Shoot. Glenn would know this. What I did know was that I didn't want to be this creature's snack. Hoping against hope, I strained for the faintest hint of Elvis, the voice that would herald the arrival of Potter's meat truck—and in this case, my only possibility for a nick-of-time rescue. No Elvis, though. Potter and that pompadour-topped crooner were probably out stomping blue-suede circles in cornfields.

I was on my own.

"Uh, well . . . I guess I could come later today, if you want. . . ." I babbled like an idiot.

"Fantastic!" Oswald Bean hippy-hopped and clapped his fleshy hands. His mini monster's stubby tail trembled even more wildly. Or maybe it wagged. Either way, the devil beast seemed excited—it probably thought it was about to lock its chomps on a purple-haired snack. *Yum, grape.*

"Gotta keep the voters, er, customers happy," Oswald

144

Bean said. "I'll switch shifts again so I'll be behind the counter. See you there! Come on, Sugar, that's a good girl."

Sugar? That hellhound's name was Sugar?

No doubt about it, nothing was what I thought it was anymore. Not a ding-dang, spoonful-of-sugar thing.

❖ ❖ ❖

I'd vaguely hoped to spot my dad on the streets that day, surfing the heat waves and pressing flesh with his adoring fans. But that didn't happen. Now here I was, about to kick off my encore performance at the Oswald Bean Fried Food Theater. Life was truly wonkers.

Roy was at my side. I'd stopped by Dante's earlier, thinking maybe I'd find Glenn and maybe talk him into coming with me for moral support. I wasn't sure I could do this without him—he's Glenn, my rock. At least he used to be. But he wasn't at Dante's. He and Burt were probably in the plant. I refused to cross the threshold of that charred bomb shelter again, even if it was to look for them. I was stupid, anyway, to think that Glenn would be moping around Dante's, waiting for me. He and Burt were probably having a lovely time together, without That Monalisa Kent Girl.

Roy had been there in Dante's instead. I found him hunched over the low coffee table, slathering pink paint across the backs of the rearview mirrors that he'd toted in that box last night. Dragging the goopy paintbrush back and forth, he'd looked as happy as a kindergartner with finger paints. No wonder Glenn was AWOL—he was only interested in Roy's car art when it involved welding. In Glenn's macho mind, pink paint could never compete with a big blowtorch. Pink was Margarita's signature color, though, so I had a sneaking suspicion this project was for her. She was always complaining that Roy was being sexist by turning cars into masterpieces exclusively for Dante's. Why the special treatment for Tuck? Didn't *she* appreciate art and cars, too, for crying out loud, *ay-ay-ay* and all that? It looked like Roy was finally cranking out something special for her. He'd already punched more than a dozen holes in the ceiling over the Pink Cloud's lounge area—I could only imagine the pink car parts had something to do with that.

As busy—and content—as he was, though, he'd been more than happy to set aside his brush to accompany me tonight. In fact when I briefed him on my plans, he'd revved himself up into quite a tizzy, as if I'd said I was booked for the *Tonight Show* or something. His left eyelid even jigged around. I'd never seen a facial tick in real life before. But then again, this was the first time I'd seen Roy so excited about something besides cars and his art book. It put Burt's hyperenthusiasm about everything to shame. I had to say, though, it was kind of cool that I was the cause of it.

So here we were, me and Roy and his break-dancing eyelid, peering through the glass windows, straining to see if there was anyone we knew inside the restaurant. Hard to say—the place was full. Five people waited at the PLEASE WAIT TO BE SEATED—THANK YOU!!! sign, and only one table was empty—right in the center of the restaurant. It was roped off with yellow police tape. None of the diners that we could see silently gnawing their fries and burgers looked familiar, not even the frazzled lady who kept stuffing and restuffing napkins into the collars of three squirmy toddlers wearing matching baseball jerseys and identical ketchup-smeared smiles.

"Man, it's packed in there." Roy turned from the window and crouched down with his back against the wall. His knees were almost in his ears. "Word spreads fast around here."

"What do you mean? Did you tell people I was doing this?"

"Only Potter." He smiled, looking very satisfied with himself.

"Roy!" Telling Potter was the same as running an ad in Times Square.

"Just remember what I said. Run in there like you own the place."

I nodded. "Like I own the place." Then a butterfly swooped in my stomach, followed by a second and a third. "You sure you don't want to come in with me? You don't have to do anything, just be in there."

"Nuh-uh, this is your deal. You need to push your own comfort threshold. I can cheer you on from here.

Just hit that empty table in the center like you've done it before."

"I have." So why didn't it feel easier?

"There you go. You already have a taste for it." He peeked through the window again, then dropped back down. "Okay, it's now or never. Ready?"

I breathed deeply twice, then set my jaw. "Ready as I'll ever be. . . ." I pushed back from the window and—wait! Who was that emerging from behind the counter with Oswald Bean? It couldn't be. . . . I pressed my face against the window again. Shoot, it was. Shaking hands with Oswald Bean was Selina Nashashibi. And next to her, of course, was George—with his camera.

Ay-ay-ay.

10

I had no idea what to expect as I threw open the doors of my first official gig. Cheers? Jeers? Painful physical retaliation? Whichever way it went, I figured it would at least start with the element of surprise. I just didn't realize that the surprise would be my own.

When I saw Selina and George with his camera, I almost chickened out. Then I remembered yesterday's walk home and this morning's breakfast raid and how good it felt to be in the driver's seat. I liked being the one who decided when and where and what the world saw of me. That's why I was here tonight with my face pressed against the window. And if I breathed a little life into these dull-eyed diners along the way, all the better. They came for a reason—maybe they were actually interested in what I had to say. I wasn't going to let a camera scare me off. *Film away, Georgie Boy. May your lighting be bright and happy, Selina.*

One last, deep breath, then I shoved open the glass door and darted for the roped-off empty table in the center of the dining area, not far from the messy baseball triplets. No sense leaping atop an occupied table—after all, stomped fries do not best friends make. This time I wore jeans, having learned my lesson about skirts and tabletops from Peeping Burt. I'd inked bumper sticker sayings up and down the faded denim with purple marker: **IF YOU DON'T LIKE THE NEWS, GO OUT AND MAKE YOUR OWN,** from the "Change the World One Car at a Time" line; **CHANGE IS INEVITABLE, GROWTH IS OPTIONAL,** from the "Drive 'Em Crazy" line; **I BRAKE FOR BURGERS AND MAYORS NAMED KLUNKEN,** from Mayor Klunken's election campaign.

George reacted to my grand entrance first, swooping his camera up to his shoulder faster than a gunslinger at high noon. Selina was mighty quick herself, whipping her microphone out and jabbing it toward dining central as I threw my arms wide, cleared my throat, and . . . saw my dad stroll out from a doorway marked RESTROOMS.

I froze.

My dad froze, too. I guess he didn't expect to find his daughter standing on a tabletop with her arms open wide and her mouth open wider. His eyebrows were arched higher than the giant yellow *M* outside. His hand hadn't moved from where he'd been giving his fly one last check for good measure.

He said nothing.

I said nothing.

The diners said nothing.

In the Nothingness, I sensed eternity slothing by, contradicting the second hand that loudly whirred around the wall clock. The only other sound was the inner tick of my brain as it flicked to Empty, a synaptic tank filled to the brim with Nothing—Nothing to say to the crowd, Nothing to say to my dad, Nothing to say to anyone about anything. It was Selina's interview all over again.

Only worse. This time I'd made a plan. I'd scoured my bedroom walls for hours, selecting just the right phrases and sentiments, strategizing exactly what I'd say and how I'd say it. All for Nothing. At my dad's unexpected entrance, every witty and wise stickerism I'd selected to show the world just who That Monalisa Kent Girl really was had fluttered right out of my mind and scattered on the floor like cards in a game of Fifty-Two Pickup.

God, I hate Fifty-Two Pickup.

That flash of anger felt good. Familiar. So I embraced it, drew upon it for energy. In spits and spurts, then, my brain synapses started reconnecting, and the scattered cards reshuffled. Phrases from my walls filtered into my consciousness in random, totally senseless pieces.

I brake for . . . The more people . . . Have you hugged your . . . Kiss my . . .

The words had the shaky quality of dreams, that surreal feeling of something starting to come into focus, only not.

George's news camera rolled on, but no one seemed inclined to end the silence. Certainly not my dad. Gee, what a surprise—he was going to let me just hang here. It was up to me to grab the bull by the horns. That or just continue standing here like a tongue-tied idiot. *Well, I got news for you, Daddy-o. I'm not going to be anyone's idiot anymore. That Monalisa Kent Girl is taking care of business.*

It wasn't easy, though. I had to consciously force air out of my lungs and push it past my vocal cords. The word "brake" limped out. It was more of a croak than an actual word, really—"bra-a-ake"—but it was a start. It gave me confidence. A little. So I proceeded, slowly, *slowly,* stringing words together, one leading to the next with no set direction.

"I bra-a-ke . . . for . . . uh . . . happiness." Well. That almost made sense. I tried again. "I brake for . . . acceptance." Better. My arms were working now, a bit chicken-flappy, maybe, but working.

"I brake for . . . things I can't get in motion." Okay, not Shakespeare, but heck, it was a solid statement.

I locked eyes with my dad, and the next few words came easily. "Give me a break."

On a roll, I pulled my eyes away and forged on, my voice louder now. "I gave him my heart, he said I'll be back." The strings came faster now, almost tumbling. "I said have you hugged your kid today? . . . Have you hugged your job today? . . . Have you hugged *anything* today?"

To stop the chicken-flapping, I wrapped my arms around my body, practically hugging myself. On my left, flustered Triplet Mom sighed, laid down the wad of napkins in her hands, and wrapped her arms around the two nearest toddlers. Seeing that, I felt a rush. My words had meaning for someone. After years of sticker collecting and memorizing and wondering why I bothered with it all, the words coming out of my mouth were familiar to me, only now I was putting them together in my own way, making my own meanings—like Burt with his words of the day. And someone else was connecting with that. It felt good. I only wished Glenn was there to see me. But he wasn't.

I locked my eyes on my dad's once more. "Have a hug today," I said to him. And then to the entire restaurant, "Have a nice day."

At that moment the buzzer on the fryer sounded, snapping me back into the real world just as a dozen fleshy slaps hit my eardrums. Instinctively I braced against the impact. But just as quickly as I flinched, I recognized the fleshy slaps as the sounds of clapping. The diners were applauding. Triplet Mom was even whistling now, two fingers to her lips and one arm trying to hug the third child across the table.

153

Good thing I'd braced myself, though, because a few French fries thwacked my forehead. No serious cranial damage, but I got the message: Not everyone was thrilled to have their meals interrupted with some weak poetic interlude—it didn't even rhyme, for crying out loud! One very agitated lady was making sure Oswald Bean got that point at the top of her scritchy voice.

None of that mattered to me. Firmly lodged back in reality, I climbed down slowly. A hand patted me on the back. Another shook my hand. A man's deep voice filtered in, grouching, "What the hell was that? I was trying to eat!" I saw none of their faces. I saw only my dad's face. His expression was slack, beaten down. The old, moldy Dad was back.

I plodded past him, each step heavier than the last. He dutifully fell into line behind me, right out the door and around the back of the restaurant. Only then did I turn and try to speak to him. I opened my mouth, but nothing came out. Big, fat Nothing. Then I tried again. This time it worked: "I know what happened."

" 'What happened'?" The words were as slack as the lips that formed them.

"Yes, what happened. That night. The fire. I know you started it. Not me. You."

At that, he deflated. At least that was how I viewed his reaction to my verbal blow: deflation. The thing is, I sort of expected it. Deep down I'd always known my dad was capable of complete deflation, even destined for it. He'd been slack and boneless for so long. I spent my whole life worrying that the miniscule piece of his consciousness in which he acknowledged my existence would crumple in on itself and be lost to me forever. Now it was happening.

"I'm right, aren't I? *You* burned down the plant," I said.

He didn't answer right off.

A terrible smell filled the pause. Only then did my nose notice what my eyes had failed to register: I'd stopped us right next to a smelly Dumpster. One that rustled. Rats, probably. Disgusting. But completely appropriate.

Then my dad mumbled something I almost didn't hear. Almost. He said, "It was so awful, Mona. She left and it was so awful."

"Who left?"

"Your dear momma. She left me and I had nothing."

"She *died,* Daddy. You had *me.*"

"She took my soul with her. I'm just a shell." More souls and shells. Had he been hanging out with Binny? I was starting to feel like a taco shell myself—all brittle and cracked. Maybe there was something to Margarita's Food Wisdom after all.

"What does this have to do with blaming the fire on *me?*"

"I was trying, Mona, really trying." His head drooped to his shoulders, his shoulders sagged to his knees, his knees slipped to his shoes. . . . "One futon. That's all. One

155

great futon, one new creation, and I'd get through it. I knew it. But I couldn't do it, Mona. I couldn't do it. Not without your dear momma . . . my muse. There I was, with the blowtorch and that metal rod and no inspiration. . . . It broke my heart all over again. I couldn't see from all the crying and I didn't see what I did with what and then the next thing I knew there was heat and flames and smoke and screaming and I tried, Mona, I tried. . . ." His voice cracked as his vocal cords began their slip downward.

"But you told everyone *I* did it."

"*I* never said you did it. The fire chief said you did it. I just . . . didn't correct him. You were only six. No one holds things against six-year-olds."

"Yes they do! Dad, people hate me because they think I set that fire."

"They don't. . . ."

"They do!" Standing there, I couldn't fathom his cluelessness about what he'd made me endure. But then, I'd never really told him, had I? I'd always figured it was my own tough luck, everyone's hate being exactly what I deserved for what I'd done. No point in upsetting dear old Dad by whining to him about it. He already had too much to handle, having a dead wife and a loser kid and all. I hadn't wanted to crush him, I hadn't wanted deflation. Only, now it turns out I was innocent of the terrible deed. Now I wouldn't tiptoe around my dad's feelings or protect his sensitive sensibilities. Now, as far as I was concerned, my dad could deflate until there was nothing left of him but a pile of limp skin and bones.

With all the venom I could muster, I hissed, "Everyone thinks you're some big hero, but you're not. You're a big coward."

I glanced back only once as I stalked away. My dad was as crumpled as the trash in the Dumpster.

❖ ❖ ❖

Tuck's needle buzzed monotonously and his mouth hummed just as tunelessly. He was in his happy place, injecting a silky shade of green into a biker's back, adding the first bits of color to the viper he'd lovingly outlined a month before.

Chet moved nimbly around the master and his canvas, ducking in and out of cabinets, restocking surgical gloves and ink bottles at each work station.

Wally emptied the autoclave a few feet away, visually inspecting each bag of shiny sterilized needle bases before storing it for later use.

I found the daily routine of Dante's comforting after my anything-but-routine day. I could just sit there and not say anything and no one would bug me about it. Soon the evening crowd would start filtering in, and I'd lose myself in the tattoo debates, their meat route gossip, the comfortable chatter about nothing and everything.

Dante's was my haven. The only other place I felt so safe was my bedroom, and now that was ruined. After I realized my dad had set the fire, I'd gone into my stickered sanctuary looking for answers, or comfort, or something, but got nothing. I'd had to turn to Margarita to try to understand. It was so amazing how she dropped everything for me. And how calm I'd felt afterward. I may not have a mother, but I had a wannabe mom.

To sit in Dante's was to regroup, so sit there I did. Calmly, quietly, almost meditatively. I even moved down to the ground and pretzeled my legs like Binny. Chet and Wally were used to me hanging around, so they didn't pay me any attention except to step around me. At one point I took a deep breath, meaning to expel it slowly and deliberately, when something on the floor by my knee caught my eye: a splotch of pink paint. I jolted to attention, swallowing the air instead of expelling it.

Roy!

The swallowed air escaped in a whopping belch.

I slapped my palm to my forehead. I'd totally forgotten about Roy, hadn't given him a second thought after spotting my dad. Here the guy had gone and dropped what he was doing to be a one-man Mona Kent cheer squad, and I'd totally abandoned him. *Nice, Mona, real nice.* Was there anyone left who I *hadn't* run away from?

I got up, grabbed my skateboard, and hurried toward the Hole. But I stopped myself before I reached the doorway. What was I thinking? Roy wasn't some lost toy. He wouldn't still be sitting in the last place I left him, just waiting for me to come and reclaim him. He wasn't at

Dante's, so maybe he'd gone to the auto wrecking yard. Or maybe he'd gone home. Or, I don't know, maybe he went someplace else entirely. What I *did* know was that it would be stupid to go hunting around for him. So I sat back down on the floor and pretzeled my legs again. What else was I supposed to do?

About a half hour later, he strolled into Dante's. I scrambled up. He didn't look mad. He looked kind of pleased, actually. But I greeted him guardedly. "Hi, Roy. Sorry I left. I was kind of distracted."

"Did you leave? I didn't notice."

Touché. A very fair response. In fact I had to admire Roy's spunk. Glenn would've chewed me out or got all pouty. Maybe there was more to Roy than a beaky goatee and an art book.

"Where were you, anyway?" I asked.

He twisted his fingers around his gelled goatee to make sure it was still pointy, then grimaced and flicked away a greenish chunk before replying. "In the Dumpster."

"In the Dumpster? I thought that was a rat!"

"Nope, it was me. I found this." He held up, like a trophy, the top half of an old-style hair dryer, the kind ladies used to sit under in the 1950s.

"You do know that's not a car part, don't you?" I said.

He knew. But he didn't care. As he explained it, when he dove into that Dumpster, the wealth of fascinating nonvehicular treasures at the bottom had surprised and inspired him. Dumpster diving was not something he'd planned to do, but it was certainly something he planned to do again. "Creativity is about seizing the moment and the idea as it strikes you," he said. "I knew I was in the wrong place at the wrong time when you and your dad came my way, so I dove for cover, and the Dumpster was the nearest vacancy. Then I didn't want to eavesdrop, so I looked for something to put my head in so I wouldn't hear." There he paused. "But I heard anyway."

Maybe I was supposed to talk here, but I didn't.

Then Roy did something that tilted my off-kilter world another seven degrees—well, not *right* then, actually. First he bent down and set his hair dryer on the ground. Then he did the amazing thing: He raised up straight again, eyeballed me warily for a moment, then quickly flung his gawky arms around my head.

I was shocked. Violence was the last thing I expected from Roy, especially since ditching him had been an accident. But there he was, mashing my nose and mouth into the yellow smiley face, trying to suffocate me against his T-shirt! Although . . . he wasn't squeezing that hard, really. In fact it was more of a light headlock than a suffocation. . . . In a flash of insight, I realized what was really happening: Roy was hugging me.

Another flash of insight: It felt good. Very good.

But the embrace ended as quickly and unexpectedly as it began. Maybe because I forgot to hug back, Roy dropped his arms abruptly and stepped away as if afraid I'd sock him in the breadbasket.

"You know," he said, "with that bunched-up expression on your face, you look just like your dad did when I crept past him at the Dumpster."

He picked up the hair dryer again and held it between us, cocking his head to the side to regard his new treasure. "It's sad, really. Someone thought this thing was broken and threw it out. Just abandoned it in a Dumpster. Like once it didn't work the way they wanted, it was no good." He rotated it slowly, admiringly. "Too bad, because in the right hands, with the right eye, it could be something else entirely. Maybe even something better."

Then he turned and left. Down the street he marched, the hair dryer propped against his shoulder like a rifle at rest, his head held high and proud. A burger wrapper hung limply from the back of his saggy black jeans.

From the doorway, the Plymouth Knight and I watched him go. We stood there for a long time, me and the tall metal sentry. Somehow I had a niggling suspicion that Roy hadn't been talking about the hair dryer at all.

11

I waited until I thought my dad would be long asleep before I snuck into the house. It turns out that stalling was exactly the right thing to do, because when I crept through the door, the bar stool was right there, like he'd waited for me before finally giving up and crashing on the futon. That would've been a joy, having to talk to him. What was there to say? Tiptoeing as quickly and quietly as I could, I moved up the stairs and slipped into my room, gently closing the door. Not a peep from downstairs. Then I turned to find a huge bowl of meatballs on sticks next to my pillow with an index card taped to the bowl. I stepped closer and read the scrawled pencil on the card: *I'm sorry*. I locked my door and vowed never to unlock it again. Good thing my mom planted that elm in the front yard when my parents bought this house. It probably made a safer ladder than bedsheets tied together and dangled out the window.

I didn't see my dad the next morning, either. I was up and out of there before he even stirred on the futon. At least I don't think he'd stirred—I went out the window so I didn't actually see him.

It was weird being up that early in the summer. Normally, if I didn't have school to report to, I wouldn't even be conscious until eleven a.m.—at the earliest. But there I was, at five-thirty in the morning, roaming the streets. The sun was rising but the moon hadn't set yet, and there was a little coolness in the air. In another couple of hours, it would be all swelter again, but for now, I actually wished I had on jeans and long sleeves. Early morning smelled weird, too, kind of plain. Maybe because the fryers hadn't been fired up yet around town, and the air's greasy French fry quality wasn't in full force.

Some crazy joggers plodded past me as I skated to I didn't know where. Without daytime hubbub and noises, my wheels sounded especially loud, click-clacking over the sidewalk cracks and crunching burger wrapper litter. I skated past the climbing tree and the Billy's Burgers picnic site. Billy's grill was chained to a metal post and the blankets were gone, but the tarp was still stretched between the poles and tree like a high trampoline, just waiting for happy picnickers to arrive in a few hours. I stopped and sat on a bus stop bench in the silence.

A squatty flattopped kid in a red, white, and yellow striped shirt wandered up and plunked onto the bench next to me. "Hey, you're that Monalisa Kent Girl, aren't you? I saw you on TV last night."

Great, just what I needed. "Two nights ago," I snapped. *At least get your facts right before you hate me on sight.*

"No, last night. Selina Nashashibi did a thing about your performance yesterday. You didn't see it?"

See what? Then I remembered George standing next to Oswald Bean and Selina with his camera yesterday afternoon. She must have put together a segment using that footage—and not bothered to even try to interview me before she aired it. "It doesn't matter. I was there. I know how it went."

He took a pack of Life Savers from his shirt pocket. "Want one?"

"No, thanks."

"You know, my aunt was a street corner poet once—in San Francisco; that's where I just moved from. But I never heard of anybody raiding restaurants before. That's what Selina Nashashibi called it, right, a poetry raid? You run in, take over, and run out again, right? Man, *everyone* watches Selina. You're lucky she discovered you."

164

"She didn't *discover* me. I just did it one day. I discovered myself."

"Still, you're lucky. Are you going to do it again?"

"I don't know."

"Good. Do it on a weekday when we open. That's my shift."

"Get up this early again? I don't think so."

"Come on, I have to see this in person. I bet the manager didn't like it. Oswald's a dink. He made me cut my hair. Hey, you think I could join you sometime? Anything that bugs him is okay with me. And I could stand being on TV. Oh, here's my bus."

He offered me the Life Savers again. This time, I took one.

Yum, cherry.

The bus rumbled to an idling stop, its air brakes squealing shrilly. As the flattopped boy climbed into it and flashed his pass to the bus driver, I noticed that the meal deal ad on the side of the bus was graffitied with purple spray paint—CONTROL YOUR DESTINY! My blue eyes widened in surprise. *Who did that?* Then the boy added to my surprise by turning, smiling, and waving. At me. That Monalisa Kent Girl. It wasn't until after the doors closed and the bus drove off that it occurred to me that I should have waved back—or at least smiled.

I remained on the bench for a while, trying to make sense of what was happening in Muessa Junction. There I was feeling as low as I'd ever felt, and there Junctioners were getting vocal and rebellious and alive. And they were using my words as their rally cry. Me, the girl who never spoke up because I knew no one would ever listen.

When two men in business suits and carrying briefcases showed up, I left my bench. Morning bus commuters weren't my kind of crowd. Not that I knew where to go instead. I couldn't go to Dante's, or to the Pink Cloud. They weren't open yet, of course. The Glenns had probably fallen asleep only a couple of hours before. Maybe I could find Roy at the auto wrecking yard. Would that kind of place be open in the morning? Not that it mattered anyway—I didn't know where Pennyworth Auto Wrecking was. What did people do this early besides jog and ride buses?

I decided to go see Binny. I hoped he wasn't still sitting on the sidewalk outside his shop, but I had a feeling he was. Maybe he'd want company. I'd stop at the market and get him a bag of donuts and some juice.

Mayor Klunken Park was on the way, and as I passed I noticed that the Muessa Junction High cross-country team was there stretching after a summer workout. One of the runners called out and waved her arm like she wanted me to come over. I probably should have kept going. That's what I normally would have done. Only, no one had ever called me over before. Certainly not Mary Lane. And lately all I seemed to do were things I wouldn't normally do.

Picking up my board, I stepped off the sidewalk into

the dead grass and walked toward her, trying to look cool instead of weirded out. She met me halfway. Several other runners came over and grouped around us.

"I saw you on TV," she said.

Mary Lane had never talked to me before. Ever. "Yeah?"

"My mom said someone should lock you in your room. That you're nothing but trouble. Rocking the lifeboat will only make it sink."

I knew I shouldn't have come over. Always trust your first instinct. I turned to leave, but some guy I didn't know was standing right behind me. Way close. Too close. "Where'd you get the idea?" he asked.

"Who cares where?" The guy next to him answered before I could. He had a friendly smile, but I didn't remember seeing him at school. Not that I ever looked around class enough to recognize anybody. I was usually slumped as low in my desk as possible. "I was there yesterday, Monalisa. I saw you in person. Me and my sister thought it was funny how you shook things up. It's so boring here. But my dad, he hated it. At least you made him look up from his stupid newspaper, though. I couldn't get him to listen to me if I jumped off a bridge screaming at the top of my lungs."

"Get real, Paul," Mary Lane said. "Parents don't listen to teenagers unless teenagers *make* them listen. No one around here does. They expect us to live the same brainless existence they chose."

I was surprised Mary Lane would say something like that. I'd assumed all she thought about was shoes and lipstick. *Shoot*—I wasn't supposed to assume.

"You need to do a poetry raid with Monalisa," she said, "and get on TV." She put her hands on her hips and jutted her chin at me. "I want to, too."

"But it's not about getting on TV," Paul said. He turned to me with his kind face. "Is it, Monalisa?"

Mary Lane snorted. "Everything's about being on TV."

The coach rushed over. "People, people, we're running a practice here. Unless you've joined the team without my knowing, Monalisa Kent, you can just move along. This isn't the time or place for your rantings. Don't you have a fire to set somewhere?"

Mary Lane laughed, then covered her mouth quickly.

I pushed past the Paul guy and stalked across the grass back to the sidewalk, threw my board down, and jumped on it at a run. I wouldn't join anything with Mary Lane in it if you paid me a million dollars. No wonder I'd assumed the worst about her. Paul, though, he didn't seem so bad. . . . Too bad his dad was such a winner. As I leaned into a tight turn around a cement planter box filled with dead weeds, I pictured my own dad sitting on his stool holding a big bowl of meatballs and an index card with *I'm sorry* scrawled on it. What did he expect me to do, say, "That's okay"? It wasn't okay. But then, all I'd ever wanted was for him to pay attention to me, and what do I do when he does? I tear him to shreds. How was I supposed to follow that up? How did I *want* to follow that up?

"I got news for you, Paul," I mumbled to myself. "The hard part isn't making them listen. It's knowing what to tell them when they do."

Sure enough, I'd found Binny on the sidewalk outside his shop. He didn't want to talk or eat or drink or anything. So I just sat there awhile, facing him, telling him about yesterday and Selina's second show and about the kids I'd run into that morning. Maybe he didn't hear me or maybe he didn't care, or maybe it didn't even matter. He just stared over my shoulder at the plant. Eventually I just gave up and left. I propped the donut bag against his right knee and set the juice by his left. Maybe he'd be in the mood for something later. The juice would probably go bad in the heat, though. Next time I'd bring him a cooler, fully stocked.

Binny might not have been hungry, but my stomach was growling, so I bought some tacos at Juana's Taco Shop around the corner. The girl at the register smiled real big when I walked up to order four soft tacos, hold the tomatoes. But her tight-mouthed manager lady moved around from the kitchen area and stood next to her looking all stern and witchy until I left with my food. I guess she didn't share Oswald Bean's opinions about the benefits of performance art. Like I would waste my time on a table in her taco shop anyway. It was empty most of the time because they couldn't get an order right to save their lives. I had to pick tomatoes out of my tacos when I sat down in the bucket seat at Dante's.

It had been lunchtime when I walked into the Pink Cloud, which had just opened. I'd cut through the Hole to find Margarita, Tuck, Chet, and Wally, but no Glenn and no Burt. I had kind of . . . sort of . . . distantly hoped to find Glenn there. He'd probably have some interesting theories about my dad and the cross-country team and girl at the register and the pineapple lover in the truck and the flattopped kid at the bus stop and Billy's budding picnic empire. . . . Jeez, it was getting weird around here. But Glenn wasn't on his futon. He wasn't in the Pink Cloud, either, and nobody knew where to find him. I had a theory about where he was. Burt was probably in there with him, the both of them painting more comic book hieroglyphics on the walls and chanting ooga-booga stuff in caveman loincloths.

With nothing better to do with my afternoon, I hung out with my tacos and Tuck's new magazines while Chet and Wally ran stuff through the sterilizer. It made a low hum, like when a computer's on—the kind of sound that's easy to tune out until its not there. Today, though, I couldn't tune it out, so I flipped on the radio. The drums and guitars were just as annoying as the hum, so I hit one of the preset station buttons. Margarita's *músico latino* station came on. The song was slow and melodic, not anything like the wild hat dance stuff we'd heard the other day on that station. I couldn't understand any of the lyrics, so I just listened to the man's voice. It was deep and soft and soothing. I went back to my bucket seat and closed my eyes.

I snapped out of my nap at the sound of Roy's loud voice just behind me. "Afternoon, gentle knight." He was talking to the Plymouth Knight in the doorway. Then he stepped in and saw me and smiled. "Well, well, you did it again, Monalisa Kent. I caught Selina's segment last night. You guys are practically best friends now."

I rubbed my eyes. Two stories in one weekend. . . . Selina was having a field day with me. "That's right, Selina and me, we're like two peas in a pod." *Best friends* . . . I didn't know what that was anymore. "Wanna come to our next slumber party?"

"I'll have to buy some face cream and curlers first." He went over to the futon and pulled the box of pink mirrors out from under it. He tossed in a huge bag of sequins. "You know, Mona, if you're planning to keep at this poetry thing, you should think about taking some poetry classes at the university next year. Sometimes they let kids do that in high school."

College classes? Glenn wouldn't have suggested college classes to me. Ever. Roy was way off target with my academic prowess. Poetry classes—ha!

"Why's everyone calling this poetry?" I said. "I

171

wouldn't know a poem if it bit me in the butt. I just said some stuff I wanted to say, that's all. It didn't even rhyme." I put my comfy work boots on the table, crossing them at the ankles. Seeing the torn eyelets on the top of the left boot, I realized how naked and raw my boot looked without a bumper sticker wrapped around it. I wouldn't wear one ever again. Bumper stickers stopped being a source of comfort for me yesterday, when they let me down after I realized my dad's treachery. No more ready-made truths and easy insights. I was now discovering truth for myself—and it was anything but easy.

I crossed my arms. "And who says I'm going to do another raid, anyway?"

He pulled his art book out of his back pocket and held it out to me. "Poetry is art, and art is anything that affects someone in a special way. Here, read the introduction." I kept my arms crossed. He put the book back in his pocket. "Do what you want. But if you do decide to go again, let me know. I'll go with you. It would be fun."

"Really, you think it's fun?"

"Don't you?"

I thought about that a second. "Fun" wasn't the word I'd use. "Liberating," maybe. And "powerful," I guess. I mean, I liked that people paid attention to me because they thought I was interesting instead of because they thought I was the devil incarnate. It was a nice change, being in control of the stares. And voicing my own feelings instead of memorizing them off a sticker made me feel real and alive and invincible. Yes, "powerful" was a word I'd use, definitely. Just thinking about grabbing the reins made my pulse quicken. So I guess "exciting" was in there, too. I uncrossed my arms. "It's a lot of things. You'll come with me, if I do another one?"

"I said I would."

Yes, he had. And I was beginning to realize that Roy only said what he meant. But what he was asking . . . I don't know, it was empowering, yes, but how long would people let me mouth off before they got militant like that Wienerschnitzel guy? "I'll think about it."

He studied me a moment; then a sly look crossed his pointy, little boy face. He dug a pen out of his pants pocket, and then a small notepad. He wrote something on the pad, tore out the page, then folded the paper in half once, twice, three times. He tossed the paper into an empty Burger King cup lying on the table and put on the plastic lid. He handed the cup to me with a pleased smile.

"You're weird, Roy."

"Just open it."

I removed the lid and pulled out the paper. *Well-behaved women seldom make history.* I looked up at him in surprise. "How do you know about this?"

"I read your boots," he said. "They always make me think. I especially liked your 'Yin to My Yang' series. You could make a lot of people think, Mona. God knows this town needs a new thought or two—or seven."

It was my turn to study *him.* I'd been hanging out in

the same place with this guy for nearly a year, but I barely knew him. He was the one making *me* think. "You should be doing these raids, not me," I said.

He laughed. "It's not my style. I'm a sculpture man; my work is behind the scenes. You're the one who craves an audience."

I snorted, sounding like Glenn. "Audience? I hate it when people stare at me."

"And that's why you dye your hair . . . and wear bumper stickers. . . ."

"Those are disguises." My eyes dropped to my naked boot. For years I'd wrapped it with stickers that suited my mood or thoughts each day so that if Junctioners said anything to me when I left the safety of my room or Dante's, I wouldn't have to talk to them to tell them how I felt. But now that I wouldn't wear bumper stickers anymore, I'd either have to speak up or forever hold my peace. "You really think they'd listen?"

"They already have."

I took a deep breath and looked around Tuck's cozy, familiar shop—the proud Polaroids on the wall, the rack of tattoo postcards and magazines and flash sets, the medieval mural on the ceiling, the hand-welded car furniture peppered about. Being here felt as natural to me as breathing. Putting myself in the public eye *on purpose,* well, that was definitely pushing my comfort threshold. But then, I'd already pushed it three times and lived to talk about it.

I folded up Roy's paper and stuck it in my pocket. "Okay. If you'll come with me . . . I'll do it."

"That's my girl! Ladies and gentlemen, the wallflower is officially dead!" He gave the box a thunderous kick, sending it back under the futon. "I'll come back later tonight and we'll plan it. There are enough fast-food joints in this town to keep us busy for months."

He promised to pick up a calendar and a map and come back after his shift at the wrecking yard. In a few hours we'd be plotting our strategy like burglars stalking an armored truck. We'd hit every burger chain in town, then work our way through pizza, chicken, Mexican, and Chinese. Monalisa Kent was about to take care of business in a very big way.

After Roy left, I got up and flicked the radio back to pounding drums and screeching guitars. Yes, "powerful" was a word I'd use. Definitely. And, heck, maybe I'd even call it "fun."

12

I snuck into my room through my window that night. And the next two nights, too. Each time, I found note cards near the bottom of my bedroom door. My dad had shoved them in sometime during the day. Every one had the words *I'm sorry* scrawled on one side. Most of them had names and numbers scrawled on the other:

Martin Wantanabe called from Burger Boy.
Ceril Benedict, Taco Heaven. Call him.
Alice Kyle from Sandwich-a-Go-Go. Call right away!

When I called the first one, I wasn't sure why I was bothering. Then I called the next, and the next, and the next, too amazed to stop. All the mom-and-pop eateries in town wanted to book me for raids, hoping they could lure customers away from the chains by providing "the hippest new entertainment." They were convinced that I would bring people in like I did for the Oswald Bean show. Me, Monalisa Kent, the girl everyone hated. It was the funniest thing I'd heard in ten years.

I should've saved my amazement, though, because the calls kept coming. WOPR Local 10 News had rerun Selina's segment about my Oswald Bean raid on all its broadcasts the next day, so everyone in Muessa Junction saw it. Must've been a slow news day. I told them all I'd think about it. What else was I supposed to say?

Then, four days after Selina's sneaky broadcast of me on Oswald Bean's table, with Roy and me still strategizing the kickoff date for my Muessa Junction Poetry Raid Tour, things went from funny to shocking. I climbed in my window around midnight to find an index card with the number for some taco shop named Rolando's down in Mesa Grande. Mesa Grande! I called the number and found the shop still open. In fact it was so busy with noisy customers that the owner had to take his phone around back to talk. It turned out that WOPR 10 had a live video stream of all its broadcasts on the Internet and Rolando saw one. Did I want to come down and raid his taco shop tomorrow night? Fridays were his biggest nights but also his stiffest night of competition, with five other taco shops within a mile of his, all vying for the same customers. If he liked what he saw tomorrow, I'd have his blessing to do periodic raids and maybe then customers would choose his shop over the others in hopes of being there when a raid struck. He'd pay me a hundred bucks each time. I'd never had any reason to leave Muessa Junction, even though I'd wanted to forever. Now I had one. I didn't even hesitate: "I'll be there."

Glenn wouldn't go with me. I went down to Dante's the next day around lunchtime after slipping a note for my dad under my door—*Gone to Mesa Grande. Back tonight.*

I caught Glenn while he was waiting for Burt. I told him about Rolando's and asked if he wanted to have some fun, just get away and be "Mona and Glenn" again. We were Forever Friends, after all.

"This is crazy, Mona. You run into places and jump on tables and totally get in people's faces when they're eating. It's obnoxious. And you're making a spectacle of yourself. I can't believe you're doing this, you of all people."

"That's just it: *I'm* doing it. No one's doing it to me. I'm in control. And most of the customers don't mind. They think it's fun. Or funny. You should come—you'll see what I mean."

"I'll stay right here. Someone has to make bail for you when you get arrested for disturbing the peace."

"I'm not disturbing anything." Well, maybe the comfortable. "The owner knows I'm coming."

Burt walked in through the Hole. "Coming where? Mona, are you doing another raid? I want to come!"

Glenn took him by the elbow and guided him to the Dante's door. "No thanks, Mona."

I watched as they headed across the street to the plant and ducked into the employee entrance. My theory was confirmed—Batman and Robin were spending all their time in the Batcave.

Roy came with me, though, just like he'd said he would. He paid Judd to take his shift at Pennyworth Auto Wrecking and drove me to Mesa Grande in his Prowler. I have to say, as much as I couldn't care less about cars, that cruiser was a pretty smooth ride. And when Roy told me all the things he'd added to soup it up—spoilers and broilers and roilers and I don't know what all—it actually sounded sort of interesting. Sort of.

"I harvested a lot of the parts from dead cars at Pennyworth," he explained.

"Dead cars?"

"Well, that's what Judd calls them, a bunch of dead cars. I'm not so sure they're really dead, though—not if you can find a way to recycle them, anyway. That's why I like using them for my art projects. No car should ever die, for in a car lies movement, in movement lies freedom, in freedom lies eternity." He hunched forward over the steering wheel and reached behind him with his long right arm, pulling his art book out of his back pocket. He set it on my lap. "That's what art is about, freedom and eternity. It's all in there."

Wow, and there I was thinking a car was just a car. Who would've guessed?

I put the art book on the floor by my feet. Maybe I would read it.

We pulled up in front of Rolando's just shy of six p.m. on Friday night. The place was a ratty shack, with paint flaking off in places and a faded menu painted right on the wall. A sliding glass window next to the menu looked out on a wooden ledge crowded with plastic utensil baskets, bottles of mysterious colored potions, and tipped-over napkin dispensers. A slab of concrete in front of the shack acted as a patio for a handful of round, plastic picnic tables with broken umbrellas. Except for a homeless guy in tattered clothes with a rolled taco sticking out of his mouth like a cigar, there wasn't anybody sitting at them.

"You sure this is the right place, Mona?"

"Yeah, it says Rolando's Taqueria on that menu."

We got out and wandered to the window. Inside, a pale cook in a grease-spattered white T-shirt and white pants leaned against a grungy stove smoking a cigarette. A hairnet covered the top of his blond hair and his eyebrows.

Roy grimaced and whispered, "This is nothing like Juana's, or Taco Bell, either." Only, his whisper was as loud as anyone's normal speech, so the cook heard him and came over.

"This is better than any stinkin' Taco Bell." I could've sworn he had a British accent. He gestured to the menu on the wall. "What do you want?"

"Actually," I said, "we're looking for Rolando."

"He ain't here."

"Oh. When will he be here?"

"When his flipping Beemer gets out of the shop." He picked up a Styrofoam cup from somewhere on his side of the dirty window, coughed up something vile, and then spit into the cup. Next to me, Roy sucked in his breath. "What do you want Rolando for?"

"He told us to come here tonight. He said Friday is your busiest night—but there's no one else here."

He pointed to the homeless man. "There's that guy. What's he, chopped liver?"

"Yeah, there's that guy. But no one else."

"Course not. This place doesn't get jumping till after eleven." He pointed his cigarette out the window to my right. "That's when everyone starts filtering out of the bars up the block. Then I can't fry up these rolled tacos fast enough."

It was my turn to take a deep breath. This was ab-solutely the wrong place. We didn't belong here. I just wanted to show the world who I was, do art and freedom and eternity and all that stuff, not be cheap entertainment for a bunch of drunks.

Roy and I lit out of there like our pants were on fire and didn't turn back. "I can't believe we drove all the way here for that," I said. "From now on, no chasing money. It takes the control out of my hands. I decide where I raid and when."

"You're not hired help."

"I'm not—I'm a raider. And raiding is all about the raid, it's not about getting paid."

"Hear, hear!" Roy thumped his big, bony hand on the dashboard. "That's where the thrill is, Monalisa Kent, in the raid. Wa-hooooo!" He let out a rebel yell, then flicked on the radio, cranking it up full blast.

I reclined the seat and stuck my feet out the open window, crossed at the ankles. The untied shoelaces of my comfy, unstickered work boots flapped in the breeze.

Yes, indeedie, cars were about movement and freedom and eternity, baby.

From then on, that's what I did: raided where and when I wanted. For the next two weeks, I raided with abandon, hitting a new place in Muessa Junction every night, getting pointers from Roy after each one: "You need to e-nun-ci-ate." "Don't make eye contact; it's confrontational." "Next time, spit out your gum first." Junctioners started laying bets, guessing where I'd show up next and waving CONTROL YOUR DESTINY! signs in the air when I did. It gave them something to look forward to, I guessed, something besides just another hamburger. Selina hired kids from my school to sit in restaurants every night and call her if I showed up. Sometimes she and George got there in time to roll some footage before I bolted, sometimes not. I didn't care. I wasn't doing this for the air time, I was doing it for me.

Besides, Selina Nashashibi and her WOPR Local 10 News crew were small potatoes. Now a national news show was doing a story on me. And they actually bothered to interview me.

Reporter: "What made you start poetry raiding, Monalisa?"

Me: "I don't know. It was just time to say something."

R: "But you say it from the tops of tables in crowded restaurants. Can't you get into trouble for this behavior?"

M: "I'm in and out too fast. And no one's getting hurt. They can just tune me out. And my friend Roy says it's free expression."

R: "How about the diners? Do they complain?"

M: "Sometimes. But a lot don't. A lot clap. They think it's fun. And eye-opening, sometimes. Which is cool. I like that, making a connection for a good reason."

R: "Why fast-food chains? Why not grocery stores, or banks, or post offices?"

M: "That's just where it started. And that's where everybody goes. Who goes to a bank?"

R: "Still, fast-food restaurants aren't known for making artistic connections."

M: "Well, they could be."

R: "How so?"

M: "Well, they already plaster their wrappers with logos and slogans, don't they? Who cares about that? They could add something useful to a meal, or at least something that makes you think. Sometimes people just need a little help getting their own thoughts jogged loose. Like with bumper stickers. I mean, if you gotta stare at the butt of a car for miles, why not have something inspirational to read, right? Same thing with burgers."

R: "You want to read hamburgers?"

M: "No. I just think that, well, they're missing an opportunity. 'Umpteen billion people served,' right? Isn't that what the sign says? What I'm saying is, they have umpteen billion moments of contact with umpteen billion customers, and all they use those for is to convince those people to come back and buy more burgers. Think of how you could change the world if you had that many people listening. But no, all they care about is chasing the money. Umpteen billion points of contact, wasted."

R: "Some would argue that the reason a business even exists is to make money. Fast-food corporations aren't social organizations. They're businesses that need to make a profit."

M: "They can do both. Think about it. You give them your money for a cheeseburger, then unwrap it and right there on the wrapper is 'Dare to think for yourself.' Or something like that. Everyone wins. People would love looking for sayings on wrappers. Something to make them

184

think. You know, like fortune cookies. Who doesn't love a fortune cookie?"

R: "So you're the verbal equivalent of a fortune cookie in their value meals?"

M: "Yeah, I guess I am, now that you say it."

The interview aired in the middle of August, just a month after my first accidental raid. I watched it on the mini TV in the Hole with Roy and Tuck and Margarita and Burt and Potter. Who knew where Glenn was. And my dad, well, I had no idea if he knew about the interview or not. I almost wrote him a note about it on an index card and slid it under my bedroom door, but then I didn't. Not that he or Glenn would've fit in the Hole anyway. I couldn't believe the rest of us did.

The interview was now the second time I'd made national TV. Aside from the magazine covers, the image of me in Binny's arms had scored major screen time ten years ago. Newspapers had picked it up, too—page A1, full color, nationwide. Funny how that works: It took me sixteen whole years to make national news as "the voice of a generation." It had only taken me six years to make it as a screwup.

The "voice of a generation" thing was Selina's doing. She called me that in her coverage of that Oswald Bean raid, and it stuck like flypaper. Actually Selina was working her way into the national eye herself—we saw her on the network newscast in a segment that aired after my interview, reporting to the reporter about how she was the first reporter to report on me.

The TV interview sparked a *Rolling Stone* interview. For three days, a *Stone*r shadowed me, writing down everything I ate and what I wore and who I talked to. I had to admit, I felt pretty cool walking into Dante's with the reporter and her photographer that first day. Burt ran to grab a pencil so that he could whip up a list of my favorite foods for them. Glenn nearly pitched a fit, though, saying he felt violated. "We're not a freak show, Mona, as much as you're acting like one."

"Who are you calling freak show, *Paco* Glenn? Why are you acting like this? Can't you just have fun with something for a change? Believe it or not, it feels good to just have fun."

"Pipe down," Tuck bellowed. "Both of you."

Margarita held up a warning hand to her husband. Seeing Tuck heel on command, I felt a little guilty. I'd used the same gesture on Glenn lots of times. "Remember, *bebitos*," she said, "all publicity for Dante's Inferno is good publicity." Then she turned to the *Stone*rs. "May I serve something? Lemonade? Soda?"

Tuck leaned down to Glenn and whispered harshly, "Go cool off."

"Why *me*?"

"Go."

Glenn ripped the pencil out of Burt's hand and threw it, then dragged him across the street to the plant. I didn't bother watching them. I knew where they were going. My guilt worsened a notch. If anyone should get kicked out of Dante's, it should be me. The place belonged to Glenn's family. I almost stopped him and said, "You stay, I'll go." But I had the reporter waiting.

The weirdest thing about the national coverage had to be that I got a call from some guy in New York City about wanting to start a "Poetry Raid Chapter."

"There's a bunch of us who want to join you," he said when I called him at the number my dad had scrawled on an index card and slipped under my door. It was a pay phone in the senior dorm at the Young Men of Peace and Faith Preparatory Academy.

"Join me? I'm not a club."

"But you could be. We'd join. We already do poetry slams, so we're good."

"Good at what?"

"At writing and reciting poetry. Don't you know poetry slams? Think open-mike battle of the poets. I won a big one last night—twenty poets were there. I actually cried real tears at the end of my poem. It was about a lost sneaker. I rocked that place."

What had I gotten myself into? Things were snowballing fast. "I don't know. . . . I need to think about this."

"Well, think fast—my friend already hit two burger joints in Manhattan. We need to get organized." Then he gave me his friend's cell phone number and made me repeat it twice.

187

That same night Mary Lane called and asked to be the cofounder of a Muessa Junction chapter with me. I thought it was a joke and hung up on her.

"It's no joke, Mona," Roy said after what had to be the tenth call asking about chapters. "Like the *Rolling Stone* reporter said, you're putting something thoughtful into a thoughtless fast-food meal. Kids are responding to that. You've hit a nerve in a generation in need of an outlet. Did you read the intro to my book yet? I highlighted the part about outlets. We've been raised on fast-food jingles and advertising campaigns; it's only natural we'd eventually start talking back in the same arena. You've helped us find our outlet, Mona."

I laughed. "You make me sound like a plug."

"A spark plug maybe."

I laughed again. Being compared to a spark plug was better than being compared to a cockroach in a nuclear holocaust. I was moving up in the world. And I had to admit, it felt good to laugh.

Not that everything these few weeks was all laughs and fancy interviews. Binny was still sitting out on his sidewalk, breaking my heart. If only I could get him to come to one of my raids. He'd be so proud. But I couldn't budge him. So I took to sitting next to him for an hour or two every morning—my back to the plant, of course. I'd keep him up to date about the world, telling him the latest about the interviews and about Dante's and the Pink

Cloud and about all the kids who were suddenly quitting the burger chains to go into business for themselves, and I'd always leave him with a goody bag full of groceries and a stocked cooler. I figured that since I had to keep restocking it, he must be eating when I wasn't around. I certainly did my best to engage him in conversation.

"Binny," I said to him one Saturday morning, "I raided Burger Boy last night. A girl who was in my Spanish class last year actually asked for my autograph on a drive-thru menu. And she asked if she could sell 'Mona Says' T-shirts. 'Mona says control your destiny.' 'Mona says listen with your mind, not with your ears.' What do you think of that?"

No response from my bumper sticker Buddha. His purple pillow was now sunbleached gray around the edges. Oddly, his leathered skin was no more sun-dried than it had been during his indoor days. It was as though his concentration had reached degrees higher than the Muessa Junction temperature, creating a force field against the waves of sunlight and heat. Like a mummy preserved for the ages, his skin remained unscathed. His spirit was another story. The man was uninterested in anything I said or brought him. The plant across the street was his focal point, and smoke was his vocal point.

"I smell it, Buttercup," he said again and again and again. That was it, that day and every other. "I smell it, Buttercup."

One time he did say a bit more. "It's calling to me, Buttercup. It's knocking on my nose, wanting in. But I don't answer, I don't answer. Oh, but it's knocking loud. . . ."

Though my sidewalk talks with Binny seemed fruitless on the surface, they did have one very useful side effect: They were making me an expert at ignoring the plant. I could sit there for hours with my back to it and almost forget it was there. Almost.

An even better bonus: That newfound ability to turn my back and almost forget was directly applicable to my daily relations with my dad.

I'd been crawling in and out of my window for weeks now. I'd managed not to talk to my dad for that long by totally avoiding him. But sometimes he made that tricky by standing at the bottom of the elm, waiting for me, holding a bowl of meatballs or a blue Otter Pop. Or sometimes he'd be holding a plate of freshly baked chocolate chip cookies. The house never smelled like cookies, though, so maybe he was getting Mrs. Teaburtle to bake them. I didn't know and didn't care. Cookies couldn't erase ten years of lying. When I saw him there I'd just drop down from the bottom branch, throw my skateboard onto the ground, and take off. With my back to him, I could forget he was there. Almost.

The hard part was getting his wild-looking eyes out of my head. They were blue and deep and he seemed to have them wide, wide, wide open all the time now, like he was in a state of perpetual surprise. It was downright creepy.

What happened to his usual futon depression? Shouldn't it have kicked back into high gear by now? I understood his change in behavior about as much as I understood Binny's sidewalk sitting. The one thing I did understand—even though I didn't want to—was the thing my dad said to me every time I found him by the tree: "I didn't know, Mona. I'm so sorry. I didn't know."

I say, his ignorance of a victim is no excuse for his crime.

Glenn didn't agree with me. He knew why I'd run that day—Margarita had told him that same afternoon. She said he came in all worried because I'd run out of the plant, so she had to comfort him. I find that hard to believe, but Margarita's no liar—or if she was, I hadn't realized it yet. Who knew who the liars were these days? If Glenn was upset, it was probably just because I'd discovered his candlelit Batcave. All he said to me about it the next time I saw him was, "Bummer about your dad." Then he turned his back and walked away from me. Sensitivity has never been Glenn's strong suit, but that was pretty pathetic even by his standards. So I didn't even bring it up with him after that—we didn't talk about my dad, we didn't talk about the candlelit Batcave, we didn't talk about my raids. We didn't talk about barely anything, which made Glenn a joy to be around when he was around. But hey, I didn't need him blowing off my feelings. I could do that just fine myself, thank you.

But the day after the *Rolling Stone* interview it did

come up. I emerged on the Dante's side of the Hole and there was Glenn, lounging Burtless under the air conditioner vent. To be honest, I almost didn't know what to say to him without Burt or Tuck there to interrupt us if things went snarky. I figured I should say something, though, to make up for getting him sent outside the day before. Nobody should ever have to heel.

Then I noticed Glenn was eating a chocolate chip cookie. A plate of them lay on the coffee table next to him. They looked homemade. Margarita hates chocolate chip cookies, so I knew she hadn't baked them. Besides, they looked edible, and Margarita's food rarely looked edible. Naturally I got suspicious. "Where'd you get that cookie?"

"Your pop."

I knew it. "He came here?"

"Yeah. He was looking for you, thought you might be hungry. He had a bowl of meatballs, too, but I told him not to leave those. They looked nasty."

I covered my face with my hands and dropped into the bucket seat. "He's too much right now." I almost stopped there, not wanting Glenn to blow me off. But Glenn was always the person I'd turned to in the past, so it seemed right to do so now. And I just plain missed my favorite confidante. That's what Forever Friends do: They confide in each other. And Glenn and I were Forever Friends, I just knew it. "I finally got my dad's attention, only now I don't want it. He's a liar."

192

Glenn waved his cookie at me dismissively. "Oh, come on. 'Liar' seems kind of harsh. I mean, technically, your pop didn't lie. He just didn't correct the fire chief."

I blinked in disbelief. "That's still lying, Glenn."

"Not technically. Anyway, see it from his point of view—really, who would hold something against a sweet little six-year-old girl?"

"*Everybody*. You've seen it yourself."

"Well, yeah, okay, they *do*. But he didn't know that would happen at the time. And maybe it wouldn't be so bad if he'd made it up to you in other ways, like doing stuff for you and protecting you, like a real dad would, instead of being such a couch potato all this time. That would have made him less of a bad guy and you wouldn't be so ticked at him."

"No, it wouldn't!" He was an idiot for even suggesting it. "And he's only admitting to it now because I figured it out. Otherwise he'd still be lying about it."

"Mona, I'm sure he's felt guilty about it all this time. I bet it's been eating away at him and sooner or later he'd have told you." Glenn nodded his head. "Yep, he was just waiting for the right time. Go easy on the guy, Mona. He's had it pretty rough."

I couldn't believe what I was hearing. Glenn and I revolved in totally different universes these days. I couldn't believe I ever thought we were Forever Friends. Forever Friends understood each other. "Whose side are you on, anyway?"

"I'm not on anybody's side. I'm just saying, your pop didn't *mean* to hurt you. Once the story got out the way it did, it wouldn't have done any good for him to fess up. People already bought the fire chief's story, hook, line, and sinker. No one could've told them different. You saw that yourself when I tried to take the blame with the Joker. You can't change what people think." He stood up, apparently done with this topic. Done with me. "You're strong, Mona. You'll get through this just fine. You always do."

He patted me on the head like a good dog, then left. I just sat there staring after him, flabbergasted. *Gee, old friend, thanks for nothing.*

13

InkFest. More circus than convention. Held every year in Los Angeles by the Occupational Tattooists & Piercers Society—"OcToPuS" to those of us in the know—this celebration of body art attracted ink enthusiasts from all over the country. The two-day convention gathered the best tattoo artists and piercers under one roof. Enticing extremists and dabblers alike, InkFest was to the tattoo world what Woodstock was to the hippies—love and peace and togetherness, man. In the hallowed aisles of InkFest booths, you'd see heavily pierced Goths breaking bread with crusty bikers, gangbangers complimenting middle-aged mommas on shoulder portraits of their babies, and plain Janes without a dot of ink on their bodies trying to figure out what the hoopla was all about. At InkFest, it was all good.

I loved it.

Tuck and Margarita were InkFest royalty. This year they were headliner emcees for the show's most popular event: the Best Back contest. Held on the first night of the show, Best Back lured dozens of human canvases onstage to bare their back tattoos and do their artists proud. The event always drew a large, rowdy audience.

Preconvention buzz had it that Back would be especially competitive this year. An amateur bodybuilder would be showcasing an original tribal design by Shaman, one of the most famous tattoo artists in the biz. Sharing the stage would be a well-loved, well-pierced, seventy-year-old librarian who would unveil the colorized version of his legendary all-black tattoo of the angel Gabriel. The most exciting rumor making OcToPuS rounds, though, was that the Guy would be debuting a new back piece in the event. It didn't matter who wore the Guy's tattoos or which category they appeared in, the Guy's work always won.

Since it was only a two-hour drive into L.A., Tuck and Margarita closed their shops every InkFest and treated their staff and regulars to a weekend of festivities. This year, I'd ride with Roy and Potter in the meat truck. ("Never know when you'll make a sale!" Potter kept saying.) Burt would hitch a ride with Glenn and his parents, and the rest of the Pink Cloud and Dante's artists would fill out the caravan with their motorcycles and tricked-out trucks. The whole gang would stay overnight, rising early the next morning to make sure we were at the head of the line when the convention doors opened.

I waited for Potter and Roy to pick me up at the Pink Cloud. It was Thursday of the last week of summer, more sweltering than ever, and a new school year loomed on the horizon like a storm cloud. If it hadn't been for InkFest, the weekend would've been pretty dismal. A pink-bladed table fan swirled the heat waves into Pepto-Bismol circles as I lay faceup on a fuzzy pink futon, my legs draped across an armrest. I was keeping an ear out for Elvis's voice, but the rest of me was focused on something else entirely: I was hypnotized by the sequined, pink-painted rearview mirrors that Roy had suspended from the ceiling. He'd made Margarita her car art, and he'd done it well.

Affixed to metal rods embedded in the overhead stucco, a dozen fist-size rectangular mirrors reflected the sunbeams that trickled in through the windows, casting a kaleidoscope of miniature spotlights around the room. It was an awesome effect that turned almost miraculous at sunset. Glenn could've explained it to me—prisms, angles, spectrums, blah, blah, blah—but that would have required him to spend more than a minute or two with me. Heaven forbid. Anyway, I didn't care about all that. What mattered to me was that every day at sunset, when the sun turned all orange and intense and hit the Pink Cloud's front window at just the right angle—about now, in fact—

I could gaze into the mirrors and enjoy distorted, wallet-size portraits of the Pink Cloud, its car posters and prissy-pants patrons, the street outside, and even the Hole and beyond into Dante's. Thanks to Roy, a garden of funhouse mirrors dripped from the sky.

Not that every idea Roy had was brilliant. No way would I risk my head in the hair-dryer stereo system he'd rigged for Margarita. The retro radio was a hit with Pink Cloud customers, though. Maybe in choosing to tattoo in the first place, they were already throwing caution to the wind. Whatever their reasons, customers climbed into the Pink Cloud On-Air Chair (patent pending, per Margarita, of course), ducked their heads under the hair dryer, and tuned in to their favorite radio stations. In the process, they tuned out the buzz of the tattoo needle. Maybe they weren't so stupid after all.

I was studying a tiny, distorted reflection of my shiny, biker-booted feet when Burt came rushing in, startling me. He had on big, dark sunglasses, and he was panicked and out of breath. "Did I miss them? I missed them! Shoot, how am I going to get there now?"

"You didn't miss anybody, Burt."

"But Dante's is locked up. The Plymouth Knight isn't even out." He scuttled quickly around the display case and raced toward the Hole.

"Burt!" I shouted, stopping him as he started pushing open the Hole's door. "Can't you read?"

He stepped back and looked down at the Do Not

Disturb sign hanging on the knob. He took off his sunglasses. "Oh. We can't go in that way, I guess."

"That's why I'm sitting in here." Really, I was basking in the spotlight extravaganza, but admitting that would sound bigheaded to the extreme. With the sun setting, though, some interesting sights were taking shape in the mirrors, and that was a solid enough reason for lingering in the Pink Cloud. "Sit down. You can't be barging in on everything all the time. Just chill."

Burt reluctantly left the door and planted his tiny tush in the empty On-Air chair. Because he wasn't tall enough to lodge his head in the musical unit, it looked like he had a big white soap bubble floating above his jet-black head.

I had to admit, I wasn't against spending a few minutes alone with Burt. I kind of missed seeing the little monkey. With all his enthusiasm and his need to try everything, he certainly would've joined in on my raids, but he never left Glenn's side and Glenn wanted nothing to do with raids—or me.

Glenn's moodiness of July eleventh had reached epic proportions. Not even Burt's idol-worship dispelled it.

Now, with only a week of summer break left, Burt was about to ship off for Texas. Glenn would take his lapdog's departure hard, I was sure. It sucked, feeling like a friend was moving on. Been there, done that. Still there. Part of me felt kind of bad for Glenn, but what was I supposed to do about it? How would I cross the icy divide even if I wanted to?

"Hey, Mona, what's up with these mirrors?" Burt was now staring at the ceiling, too. "Why did Roy hang them from the ceiling? How did he know to do that? How did he know they weren't just trash? I'm afraid to throw anything away now. I mean, how do I know when something is trash and when it's art?"

I'd almost forgotten how many questions Burt could ask in a single breath. As usual, though, his questions made me think about something I'd never even considered. Maybe I should have read Roy's art book.

"Well," I said, trying to think it through, "telling art from trash seems like something you have to decide for yourself. It's all in how you look at things, I guess."

At that we both squinted and swiveled in unison, like synchronized swimmers, to see what we could see. A hazy, pocket-size Lamborghini materialized in one of my mirrors.

"I'd say that's what Roy's car art is all about: seeing things differently," I continued.

Another mirror was a psychedelic blur of spinning fan blades and pink futon fuzz. I had to close my eyes and shake the marbles in my head after that one. "He sees the unexpected when everyone else sees the expected."

The next mirror reflected a black-bordered poster of a wilting tree against a glowing white background. No, that wasn't quite right. The Pink Cloud doesn't have any nature posters. . . . I cocked my head to the side. That wasn't a black border. . . . I used my finger to trace an imaginary line from the mirror to its target.

Huh. The mirror was aimed at the Hole. Burt had pushed the door open several inches when he tried to rush in, and with the mirror angled just so, I could see right into the tunnel-like room.

I squinted harder, making my eyes hurt.

Yep, I was seeing into the Hole. What I'd thought was a poster's black border was actually the black door frame on the Dante's side of the Hole, and the whitish glow was really the lighted tattoo shop beyond it. And that wilty tree . . . well, it had a familiar look to it, too—not that Dante's had trees, of course. . . .

I peered even harder.

Burt scurried to the futon next to me and pressed his cheek against my cheek to line up his eyes with mine. At that moment the sun finally surrendered day to night. Just before it dropped below the horizon, it shot out one last brilliant shaft of light, zapping the mirror full-tilt. In that instant of stark light, the wilting tree trunk came into focus as a bending back, its bushy foliage as shaggy hair, its saggy branch as a human arm. I recognized the bulky arm. It was Glenn's, and he was reaching out to something . . . to another tree . . . no, to a person . . . a hooded person in a tattoo chair—

Oh my God!

I ejected out of the futon, knocking Burt onto the floor

at my feet. Not that my feet were beside him for long. As soon as my soles contacted the black-and-white tiles, they beelined for the Hole. I yanked the door fully open, jammed myself into the dollhouse-size room, and popped out like a cork on the Dante's side.

My explosive entrance sparked a collective gasp. Then: "Mona, what are you doing in here!" Margarita wasn't asking a question.

"What the hell!" Tuck wasn't asking, either.

"What? What's going on?" That *was* a question, muffled as it was. It came from the hooded figure. The man—for surely that bulky back belonged to a man—was leaning, bare chested, against the chairback, his hooded head twisted in the direction of the angry cries.

My own question wasn't muffled in the least. "Glenn, *what* are you doing?"

Glenn turned swiftly. "Mona?" His surprise was conveyed as much by the arched eyebrows above his dark glasses as by his voice. He stepped toward me, a buzzing needle in his gloved hand. In doing so, he exposed a nearly finished tattoo on the man's back.

At the unobstructed, front-row view of the painted back, I gasped ten times louder than Margarita and Tuck did a moment before. The tattoo was an enormous, gorgeous, flawless human eye—wider and bluer than Superman's tights.

Clarity. That's what cold-cocked me at that moment. Clarity about what I was witnessing. Clarity that what I now saw was not a surprise after all. Clarity that, in fact, I'd known this for a long time—since I came upon the hieroglyphics in the plant, at least—I just hadn't admitted it to myself.

Glenn was the Guy.

And that was my eye flowing out of his needle.

Potter's meat truck turned out to be a surprisingly comfortable ride. Roy, Potter, and I all fit in the front cab with room to spare. And even though dangling sides of beef banged the walls in the refrigerated section each time Potter skidded around a corner, most of the drive to L.A. was freeway, so there wasn't really much meat-related noise. All in all, it should have been one lovely jaunt to the fair. But it wasn't. Glenn had ruined it. He'd ruined everything.

The guys must've sensed my mood, because they let me keep to myself. They spent the trip harmonizing with Elvis and occasionally pulling to the shoulder of the highway to do business with meat-crazed motorists. Those two were not shy, that's for sure. Left on my own, then, I did a lot of thinking, trying to figure out how Glenn could have lied to me all these years. And more importantly, why.

When I'd asked him that question back at Dante's— "Why would you do this to me, Glenn? Why? I'm your best friend, and you lied to me. Doesn't anyone tell the truth anymore? Why did you lie to me, Glenn?"—his response had been short: "Jeez, Mona, why does everything have to be about you?" That was it. Then he'd turned his back on me, choked up on his needle, and resumed poking the lifelike eye.

I'd fled back through the Hole just as Pete's Meat Wagon pulled up. Strains of Elvis mingled with the Pepto-Bismol swirls in the air. *"You ain't nothin' but a hound dog, cryin' all the time. . . ."* In the cab, Potter and Roy sang off-key and grinned like schoolboys on a field trip.

Two hours and a hundred fifty miles later, I was still clueless as Potter skidded the truck to a stop in the convention center parking lot.

I didn't gain any insight tossing and turning in a lumpy sleeping bag that night, either. Margarita believed that hotels were a waste of good money, so we all lay in sleeping bags on the cold, hard parking lot asphalt. Well, not Margarita or Potter—they called dibs on their front seats in exchange for driving. By the time the InkFest doors swung wide on Saturday morning, I was in no mood to socialize.

Usually InkFest really was a day at the fair for me: cotton candy and hot dogs, aisles of busy tattoo booths, hundreds of ink enthusiasts baring it all—well, *almost* all. InkFest had always been the high point of my year. There were attractions beyond the tattoos and circus food, too: carts with ball caps and chains, racks of backless shirts and other tattoo-revealing clothing, tables of bumper stickers and obnoxious T-shirts, counters of jewelry, and rows of piercing chairs. Every one of the packed aisles eventually converged on a stage at the head of the convention hall. Rows of metal chairs surrounded the platform stage.

The tattoo contests that took place on that stage were the highlight of InkFest, allowing people of all kinds to show off their ink. Judging categories included Best Leg, Best Back, Best Sleeve, Best Vest, Best Tribal, Best All-Over, and Best of the Day. The crowd favorite by far was always Best Back, but my personal favorite was Best Sleeve. Stretching from shoulder to wrist, a sleeve lets a tattooee show off his or her ink at all times with minimal fuss. Short-sleeved shirts or tank tops did the job well. Best of all, sleeves were easy for people to admire on themselves. No mirrors needed—they just raised their arm and there it was.

Potter's awesome keyboard-and-jitterbuggers sleeve had taken first in Sleeve five years running. It was hard to beat Tuck's handiwork. Last year was a close one, though. A sci-fi fan almost beat Potter with two arms tattooed like Borg appendages. Even Tuck admitted they looked pretty realistic. But the sci-fi geek went too far—he duct-taped drills to his hands to complete the Borg character. The purist judges ruled that too theatrical and disqualified him.

This InkFest, though, I wasn't in the mood to dive into the action. Instead I went into observer mode. I plopped myself down in a metal chair, where I could see most of the convention floor by just swiveling in my seat. For a few minutes I was joined by a chatty girl who I remembered from previous conventions. She was hard to forget, with her pussycat facial tattoo and fang-sharpened eye-teeth. But with me being a social dud and all, she didn't stay long. When she left me in search of someone more exciting, my mind flashed on an image of me sitting on the futon where my dad usually sits, shutting out the world day after day with no one to talk to. Lonely and friendless and bitter. I pushed it away with a mental *pshaw.*

I didn't push away the hot dogs that Roy kept bringing me, though. His thoughtfulness made it possible for me lag there all day, right through Best Leg and Best Vest, right through the "Piercing for Grandmas" lecture, and right through the "Fastest Needles in the West" exhibition—including Burt's attempt to join the needle-tossing finale. That was a doozy, to say the least. Three twentysomething chicks in Annie Oakley outfits ran around the stage juggling tattoo needles and ink bottles, tossing them to each other over their shoulders, under their legs, straight up in the air, all the while trading out turns buzzing a tattoo of a Colt .45 into the shoulder blade of some guy with a black ten-gallon hat. In five minutes flat, they'd completed a pretty decent-looking tattoo. When it flashed on the giant video screen, I clapped for the Annies' moxie as much as for their tattooing skills. Those girls knew how to entertain. Then they launched into a finale that was so fast and furious that I could barely follow it. Apparently Burt could, though, because out of nowhere he leaped onto the stage and tried to intercept one of the flying needles—he wanted to juggle, too, I guessed. All he managed to do was knock the needle out of its flight path and into the ten-gallon man's foot. That boy shouldn't be allowed near anything sharp.

Whenever things slowed down on the stage, I passed the time by searching for Potter's bull's-eyed head in the crowd or by straddling my chair backward to observe the two nearest booths: Shaman's tattoo booth and the Bumper Stickers for Bumper Brains booth.

Shaman was an InkFest staple and a national tattoo icon. Tall and tight like a marathon runner, he wore nothing but a loincloth. His ears, eyebrows, and nose were pierced with hand-carved wood. His head was shaved except for three beaded braids on his forehead and a blond braid that sprouted from the back of his head and curved down his back like a second spine. No one knew his true heritage, but legend linked him to a long line of medicine man ancestors. Shaman's claim to fame in the tattoo world was his mastery of traditional tribal tattooing. Surrounded by fluffed pillows, smoldering incense sticks, and the soft strains of pan flutes and birdsong, he worked gracefully, a blissful drummer lightly tapping out his tune on drumsticks of firm bamboo, a needle attached to one. With confident, rapid wrist flicks, he tapped the plain stick against the needled, driving the metal point into his customer's skin like a sewing machine. Every few taps, he swooped his needle into an inkbowl at his side, then swooped back and tapped some more. Shaman's technique dated back thousands of years to the very roots of tattooing. People who got tattoos this way called it a spiritual experience.

Not me. I was already willing to commit Potter to the nuthouse for his record-breaking electric needle sessions with Tuck. Shaman's manual technique was even harder for me to stomach. As I watched him work his sticks on a succession of customers, I was as horrified as I was fascinated. It just seemed so painful. His own face, arms, and legs were heavily patterned with the black swirls and thick, mazelike designs of his tribal style. Incense wafted to my nose. *Yum, lilac.* I felt homesick for Binny's shop and a simple life that seemed gone forever.

Bumper Stickers for Bumper Brains, on the other hand, left me feeling cold. At past InkFests, I'd spent hour after glorious hour at that booth, scouring the sticker stacks for new and thought-provoking additions to my collection. This year, I couldn't care less about them. They were just stickers, with canned sayings and as much originality as butter on toast. Today's most popular sticker was **MEAN PEOPLE SUCK**. A truly uninspired choice, in my admittedly sour-mooded opinion. Maybe I was getting like Tuck, who refused to use other people's flash tattoo templates. Maybe he wasn't just being art-snobby after all. Maybe he wanted to show the world what he could create, not what he could trace.

I was just swiveling to try to spot Chet—I wanted to

ask him if the tribal swirl around his eye was the result of stick-pounding—when the overhead lights flickered. *Rocky* theme music erupted from the sound system, and Margarita and Tuck began a slow and dramatic ascent to the stage. I was surprised to see Glenn ascending between them. What was he thinking? A million eyes would be on him. He hated that.

A deep-throated chant—"Tuck, Tuck, Tuck"—rumbled beneath the music. Fans in the front row stomped heavy, rhythmic foot stomps, tremoring the cement floor around the stage. The vibrations rippled outward under my feet. By the time the Glenns reached the podium, the entire Ink-Fest crowd had drained down the aisles and pooled in the rows of metal chairs.

Best Back was beginning.

Bookended by Roy and Potter, I watched my extended family preen for the audience. I felt oddly distanced from them, analyzing their theatrics and comparing it to my own performance style as a raider. I had to admit it, their stage presence was impressive. Margarita giggled and waved and air-kissed the audience. Tuck growled, then ripped his T-shirt to expose his famous chest tattoo: the Round Table with King Arthur, eight fork-wielding knights, and a bulging bucket of KFC's Original Recipe. And while Glenn looked rattled to be in front of so many people, his shaggy hair and the tinted glasses covering his fire-damaged eyes gave him the air of a rock star.

Tuck was the first to speak, jamming the microphone

tight against his king-size lips and dredging thunderous decibels up from his diaphragm.

"La-a-a-a-dies . . . a-a-a-and . . . gentlemen-n-n-n . . . , welcome . . . to BEST BACK!"

He put TV wrestling announcers to shame. The InkFest audience responded with a roar. Unable to resist the crowd's enthusiasm or Tuck's charisma, my icy mood began to crack. When Tuck smiled wide and swooped his enormous arm to his left to introduce his beloved wife and son, I applauded as loud as anyone. These were my Glenns.

The Best Back contestants were swept up in the rowdy mood, too. Tuck and Margarita traded off announcing the contestants as Glenn timidly read off the names of the tattoo artists responsible for the featured art. One at a time, the contestants pranced to center stage, pivoting and posing, proudly displaying their back tattoos. The crowd whistled and cheered each contestant, no matter how cool or ugly their ink. True to InkFest's spirit of openness and brotherly love, the crowd supported anyone brave enough to put themselves up for judgment. The large screen suspended behind the stage showed close-up video of the back tattoos, so that even those farthest from the stage could admire the designs.

"Ester Prinn, who has not the bird in the hand but the bird on the back, please step forward," said the lovely Margarita.

"Artist: Marco Estrella. Business: Birds of Paradise Tattoo. Location: Vista Mesa, California," read Glenn.

A peppy woman in a backless halter top glided on-stage with her arms flapping. She stopped in front of the camera and gave us a long look at the bald eagles soaring across her back. The tattoo was realistic, but otherwise nothing special in my book. The thing was, I didn't get the sense that the birds were actually flying. But then, I'm not a bird person. I clapped anyway, because Ester Prinn was pretty game to be flying around the stage like that.

"Joe Prock, show us what you got!" Tuck bellowed.

"Tribal design by Shaman, of Shaman's Hut in Vista Azul, California," said Glenn. He sounded a little more comfortable that time. Margarita kissed his cheek.

Shaman's amateur bodybuilder was a hit, of course. Bold black swirls started at his neck and rolled down-ward, spinning through and around each other, balling in the small of his back, fanning out across his wide shoulder blades. My eyes swooped and dipped with the swirls, the sound of birdsong filling my mind. The gym rat's muscu-lar posing earned him extra whistles from the girls in the audience—and from a few guys, too.

"Phil, *mijo, por favor,* come, honor us," breathed Margarita.

"Color by the one and only Shawn Jane of the Jane Gang, located in sunny Valle Vista, in California, in the good ol' U.S. of A.," Glenn bellowed. Tuck thumped him on the back proudly.

When seventy-year-old Phil's colorized Gabriel floated center stage, the OcToPuS crowd gave their oldest living member a standing ovation. The bright, mesmerizing Gabriel, backlit with a halo of gold, floated on a sky of the richest blue. His peachy hands were clasped softly over his heart, and his bottomless green eyes bathed us with love. Like enormous feathered clouds, Gabriel's outstretched wings wrapped softly around Phil's sides and shoulders. You could almost hear their gentle beats as the angel soared toward Heaven. The well-earned ovation made Phil flush with pleasure, deepening the color in Gabriel's pinked cheeks.

I could see Glenn's confidence grow with each contestant. He enunciated the artists' names more clearly and projected his voice more forcefully. His parents had their arms around his shoulders, and he was smiling wider than I had seen in months. Heck, I'd almost forgotten the guy had teeth.

I snorted to myself. *The Guy.* He sure snuck that one by me. How could I have missed it?

I looked at him then, hard. I couldn't remember doing that before. Ever. I saw him up there on that stage, proud and confident, and I knew that I was seeing him—really *seeing* him—more honestly than I ever had. In that mind-blowing moment of epiphany, I recognized the shaggy-haired boy on the stage not as My Friend Glenn, but simply as Glenn. Period. From my chair in the crowded audience, I watched him basking in the spotlight—*his* spotlight, not mine—and I was happy for him. I myself had accidentally discovered what it felt like to have eyes on you for a good reason instead of a bad one—it made you feel good, like a hero. And once you got a taste of heroic, you didn't want to lurk around in disguises anymore. Now Glenn was getting a taste of the spotlight. Only a privileged few—me and Tuck and Margarita—knew his top-secret identity, his alter ego. And it would stay that way until he wanted otherwise. We would keep his secret. *All* of us. Glenn was Batman. He was Superman. He was the Guy.

And then—*sha-blamm!*—*it* hit center stage. Glenn's—no—*the Guy*'s tattoo.

My famous eyeball.

14

I grabbed Roy's fingertips and crunched them like a vise.

"Ow, Mona!"

"Sorry." Total knee-jerk response. I didn't mean to hurt him. Good guy that he was, though, he didn't make me let go.

Then, out of nowhere, a short, skinny kid with dark glasses bolted across the stage, right past Margarita and Tuck and Glenn. It was Burt!

"Ow!" My turn to squawk as Roy crunched tight on my fingers. Squeezing those racquetballs sure made a guy's grip strong. "What the heck is he doing?"

Burt was bowling over the guy with the eyeball tattoo, that's what he was doing. Reaching center stage, Burt planted himself in front of the microphone and hollered at the top of his monkey lungs:

> *"If I had a noodle*
> *for each nickel that I ate,*
> *I'd have a pocket full of s'ghetti,*
> *and a C-note on my plate!"*

The audience stopped cheering. The contestants stopped prancing. The Glenns stopped announcing. They had no clue what was going on. I did, though: Done helping the paramedics treat the ten-gallon man and clearly excited by the sight of his mentor onstage and the yells of the crowd, our impulsive little friend had decided to seize that moment to do Glenn proud. *Carpe diem, Burto.* Monkey boy chose that moment to launch his first Poetry Raid.

At least one other person knew what was up. Ending the two heartbeats of agonizing silence that followed Burt's ode to noodles, a nerdy college kid a few feet from me with a Mark Twain tattoo on his forearm hollered out, "Poetry raid!"

The cheer-drunk crowd exploded in wild delight.

I turned Roy's fingertips completely blue. The pussycat-faced girl had just jumped onstage and was leading the Poetry Raid movement down a seedy sidestreet:

215

"There once was a man at the zoo
Whose job was to shovel the—"

Ew! I slapped my free hand over one ear. There'd be no reclaiming the show now.

15

In the billowing smoke I see only a dark, looming figure, backlit with a halo of red and orange, emerging from murky clouds and a swirling vortex of flames.

My angel.

I see my angel's arm squeeze firmly around my waist. It pins my arms as I struggle and thrash and reach for a rail that's no longer there. We float through the smoke.

Then I see the sky,

the stars,

a yellow coat,

a flash of foamy white. . . .

Where's my angel? I don't see my angel anymore.

Smoky images clouded my mind as the crowd's rowdy recitations filtered backstage where I stood, still clutching Roy's fingertips. My free arm was locked across Burt's chest, holding him protectively against me. He was staring, wide-eyed, at the stage he'd just fled, where people were grabbing the mike or just plain shouting over each other, all striving for bigger, better rhymes for "poo."

I tried to block out the potty poems, to focus instead on the memory that had erupted out of the emotions swirling inside me—the memory of my angel . . . my savior . . . my father.

Dad had saved me and Glenn, and he had battled flames and smoke to do it. I saw it all in the flashback. I saw the truth. Dad may have let me take the blame for his mistake, but when push came to shove, his instinct had been to fight for me. Dad was not a traitor, and he was not a coward, not in his heart.

At heart he was a hero.

My hero.

It was time to be as brave as Dad had been that night. If he had that in him, so did I. No more withdrawing, no more ignoring. Not for me. Not for Dad. It was time to take care of business. If I had to battle fire to do it, I'd fight my way to Dad and save him.

Save us both.

16

We returned from InkFest on Sunday afternoon to a dramatic spike in the heat wave. The streets were deserted. My fellow heat-toughened Junctioners had finally surrendered to Mother Nature and retreated indoors. But nowhere was it hotter than here, across the street from the plant, where I found Dad sitting next to Binny. They were both babbling like lunatics.

Dad was mumbling about the fire he hadn't meant to set. Binny was mumbling about the fire he hadn't been able to extinguish. Neither was listening to the other. Both were sweating. Binny's force field must be failing.

I wiped a heavy trickle of sweat from my own face.

Expecting no response but knowing I had to try to fight for my angel, I said, "Hi, Dad."

I guess Dad wasn't as far gone as Binny. At the sound of my voice, he pulled back from wherever he was in his head to join me in blistering Muessa Junction.

"Mona, you're back!" He practically screamed this. "I've got supper all ready for you. Just need to heat it up. Swedish meatballs. You love Swedish meatballs, don't you, Mona?" His speech was quick, almost frantic.

He extended a shaky arm up to me.

I looked down at that arm, all hairy and sweaty and anything but angelic. I remembered that same shaky arm holding the blowtorch. I remembered it flailing for balance before Selina's interview. I remembered it hanging weakly from the side of the Dumpster. And I remembered it locked like a vise around my waist when the rest of my world went smoky black. Reaching out my own arm, I slipped my hand into his and smiled. My angel smiled back.

The temperature of Muessa Junction dipped several degrees.

As I assisted Dad to his feet and looked toward Binny, wondering how I'd reach him, a water balloon exploded on the ground, drenching us both.

"Yee-haw!"

We turned in the direction of the shout to see Burt whooping and running at us with a second water balloon. He needed two hands to fling the humongous H_20 bomb, and when it pounded the cement, a mini tidal wave clobbered us.

An instant of shock, then I was basking in the glorious coolness of water-soaked clothes. Misty halos of steam rose up around me and Dad as the sun quickly steam-dried our wet fabric. Binny, too, had a steamy halo, but he wasn't reacting to the unexpected water show. The chilled water would probably do him good anyway.

Two more water balloons dropped from the sky. But this time they came from somewhere behind Burt. I ducked instinctively, but Burt spun into a crouch and whipped up a shield that had been slung across his back. He'd already recovered from his InkFest scare. I could only shake my head at his resilience.

"Ha, ha! You missed your prey, Dark Knight!" he shouted. "Squire Burt will not be vanquished!"

He was waving the Plymouth Knight's hubcap shield over his head. He shouldn't have bothered with the shield, though—Glenn had a terrible arm. It was amazing that his two lobs had even landed on the correct side of the street.

Shrieking like a little girl, Burt dodged behind me when Glenn followed his aerial attack with a ground charge. It sure was something, seeing Glenn lumber at us with a long metal pipe tucked against his side like a lance. The closer he got to us, the more flushed his face appeared. The mottled-red color resembled that wired, edge-of-a-meltdown flush I'd seen on kids' faces in the McDonald's playground after one too many goes on the plastic jungle gym with tummies full of apple pie. The smile that had budded on Glenn's face at InkFest was now a sunflower in full bloom. He must not have been too shaken about having had his spotlight extinguished by Burt's raid. Flushed, grinning, and loping toward us like a lame horse, Glenn looked completely ridiculous. And totally charming. I couldn't help it, I had to smile, too, as a wave of nostalgia for our carefree days washed over me. I was fighting for Dad, I could fight for my Forever Friend Glenn, too. I missed him. Why, the last time I'd seen Glenn wave a pipe and act so silly and playful was—

My smile hardened. Then it compressed into a thin, sweaty line: The last time I'd seen Glenn wave a pipe like that was when I was six and he was five—the day the plant burnt down.

As Glenn jousted past me, I stabbed out my arm and latched onto his shirtfront, yanking him to a stop. A harsh *r-r-r-i-i-p-p-p* cut the air. His lance shot loose from his sweat-drenched hand.

"Hey!" he shouted.

"You did it," I said icily.

"You ripped my shirt!"

"*You* set the fire." I was shaking with fury.

Glenn knocked my arm away and jabbed his skewed glasses back into place. Then, slowly, deliberately, he straightened to his full six feet, all the while brushing at his ripped shirtfront just as slowly and deliberately. He seemed to be bracing himself for the showdown we both knew had been coming since I discovered him tattooing my big blue eyeball into that customer's back two days ago.

But I didn't have tattoos on the brain. I had blowtorches. Specifically, my brain was looping through a sequence of images all featuring one particular blowtorch, a pipelike tool that looked very much like a lance in the bulky-yet-babyish hands of five-year-old Glenn, ten years ago.

The memory snippet that had revealed my dad's treachery was replaying itself in my head. Only now, triggered by Glenn's pipe-jousting, the *full* memory bubbled up:

Daddy crumpled on the floor in a blob of "I miss your dear momma" sobs. The welding torch—unlit!—in Glenn's hands. The flame exploding from the tool as Glenn turned the switch. Glenn dropping the torch onto the pile of futon padding at his feet . . .

"I remember now," I snarled at Glenn. "*All* of it. *You* started that fire. I saw you."

Behind me, Burt's shield clattered to the asphalt. "What?" he croaked.

Nearly simultaneously, Dad winced and bounced like a pogo stick, clutching the foot just crushed by Burt's shield.

Glenn's reaction was just as physical as Dad's. This wasn't the showdown either one of us had expected. My hissed accusation pounded him as viciously as a slap on the cheek, knocking his head back and his glasses up his forehead. His hands whipped up instinctively to shield his light-sensitive eyes. But before he yanked his shades back down, I caught a glimpse of his naked eyes, so raw, so vulnerable . . . so Superman blue.

I felt the ricochet of my verbal hand-slap in that glimpse. Until now, I'd always thought of Glenn's eyes as huge and black and sunglass-shaped. Strong, blank, unreadable. I was wrong. Those thick, dark glasses hid eyes as tormented as my own. In Glenn's blue-eyed vulnerability I saw my own fire-inflicted trauma, and it knocked me off balance. That was *his* eye on the customer's back, not mine.

I wasn't as off balance as Glenn was, though. His back was arched, his body tensed in the same pose he'd struck on the balance beam in gym class last semester, right before he back-flopped to the mat and knocked the air out of himself. This time, though, his survival instincts must have kicked in. He righted himself and said defiantly, "You're talking out your hole, Mona. You always spout off about things you don't know. You didn't see anything. You were all the way across the room, for crying out loud, playing gymnast on that stupid railing. Daddy dear needed your help, but no, *you* were off playing Mary Lou Retton."

"Shut up, Glenn!" I screamed.

"Yep, there it is, vintage Mona." His sarcasm dripped acid. "You don't want to hear it. You never want to hear it. You're *so* protective of dear Daddy, but where were you when he fell apart and cried like a little girl, huh? Where were you?"

Then Glenn lost it completely, waving his arms and stomping his feet in the steaming puddles. "*I* was there, too, you know, but nobody cares about *that*. *Nobody* cares what I have to say. *Nobody* cares that I turned off that blowtorch for him. He was just dropping it and picking it up, dropping it and picking it up. He cried like a baby the whole time, mumbling about his muse being dead and gone. *I* turn the stupid thing off and who's the hero? He is. He's the hero." He pokes his finger at Dad, then at me. "He's no hero, and neither are you. You. You. You. That's all you Kents think about. Always you—what *you* did, what *you* lost. What about me? Huh? What about Glenn? Nobody even cares that I was there. I set the darn fire, and nobody even cares that I was *there.*"

"You?" Daddy blurted, shocked.

"You?" Burt cried, horrified.

"You!" I snarled, furious.

Glenn froze. Then he blinked a few times like he'd been sucker punched. He started stammering, his words tumbling fast: "I . . . well . . . I . . . not on purpose! It slipped! After I turned it off, I turned it on to try it myself and—it was hot! All that material was on the floor and . . . and . . . it was hot! No wonder he kept dropping the stupid thing. It was hot!"

Burt came as unhinged as his idol. "No you didn't Glenn no you didn't it was an accident no you didn't. . . ."

I was ready to shred Glenn like I'd shredded Dad at the Dumpster. He'd lied to me for ten years, then he went

225

and let me blame my dad on top of that. "Oh my God, Glenn, you—"

"Stop!" Burt's desperate protest cut me off. Then he started running, looping around us in frantic circles, his cupped hands clapped to his ears. "La, la, la, la, la, la . . . !"

But I tuned out Burt's "la, la, la" and his hysterical circling and his rantings about squires and Dark Knights and damsels in distress and Batcaves. I tuned out the plant behind me, the oppressive heat wave, the entire world. I registered nothing but Glenn's treachery. The Kent family full-retreat reflex was kicking in. I didn't even care that Binny had been jogged from his reverie by Glenn's revelation.

"Poor Paco," Binny crooned. "Too young to tame the beast. Poor, poor Paco."

I felt no pity for Glenn. Here I was, ready to forgive him for his secret cave and his secret identity like I was forgiving Dad. Now, though, learning that for the past ten years Glenn had let me think that *I* had set the fire when *he* had really set it (no wonder he'd defended Daddy!) . . . why, I was back in the crushing emotional place that had landed me and Dad next to that smelly Dumpster. I—

No! No. This time I would *not* tune out the world. No abandoning anyone next to—or in—Dumpsters like so much trash. I was always running from people or ducking my head or retreating into disguise, and look where it got me. This time I would stay right here and be myself and fight for those who mattered to me.

How long it took, I didn't know, but with super-human effort I refocused on the people around me—my dad, my old friend Binny, my *supposed* friend Glenn. . . .

Wait. Something was wrong.

I did a mental head count: One. Two. Three. Me makes four. There should have been five. Who was missing? Burt. Where was Burt? He was right there a minute ago, yelling about la-la-land and Batcaves and retreating.

"Is that smoke?" Dad startled me with his question.

My blood ran cold. I spun to look in the direction of Dad's baffled gaze—the plant.

Yes, Dad had called it right on the money. That was smoke, and it was pouring out of the plant.

In nature, where there's smoke, there's usually fire.

In Muessa Junction, where there's fire, there's usually the plant.

In my tormented life, where there's trouble, there's usually Glenn and Burt. Only, Glenn was standing right next to me.

My math-crippled brain had no problems computing this logic. Even without a calculator, I knew that three "usually's" equals one "for sure": Burt was inside the burning plant.

And burning it was. Like a tinderbox awaiting its spark, that plant had morphed from sleeping giant to flaming Goliath as quickly as it took the four of us across the street to realize this wasn't a mass delusion. The plant was indeed on fire.

Again.

And this time, Burt was inside.

I screamed that fact loudly, which instantly launched Glenn toward the employee entrance at full gallop. I sprinted behind him. But we couldn't get close to the doorway because of the flames' searing heat. I swear the hairs on our arms were brittling from the toasting. After a decade of simmering, the geothermal heat that had boiled Muessa Junction so slowly from below must have finally breached the surface. The flames that spit up reached straight from Hell, stewing airborne water molecules, sizzling the air around us. With the sun pitching in its heat rays from above, my hometown was roasting like a patty on a grill.

Glenn and I, heat-toughened over the years and insanely adrenalized by fear, refused to retreat. We bolted back and forth, skirting the perimeter of the inferno, looking desperately for a way in. We probed forward when opportunity knocked, hopped back when flames blocked. Stray embers landed on our purple and blond heads like flicked cigarette butts. We merely brushed them away. All focus was on getting Burt out of that building—which meant getting ourselves in.

But we found no way in. The Batcave was out of reach. A fire-breathing Godzilla blocked the drawbridge, its flaming breath filled the mote.

Smoke had billowed skyward and fanned out, turning day into night. I had trouble seeing more than a few feet in front of me, so I knew Glenn was nearly blind in the darkness. Next to me, he angrily ripped off his tinted glasses and smashed them to the ground, cursing them and the fire that had ruined his sight so long ago.

Instantly he cringed with pain as the blazing firelight overwhelmed the damaged nerves behind his eyes. But then, just as suddenly, he stood straight as a pole, surprise on his face, his tender baby blues wide open.

"I can see? I can see!"

His chest puffed up with a surge of strength and power. Setting his expression firmly, planting his feet wide, he jammed his hands on his hips and stared down the flaming beast. Like the Fighters for Justice on his Batcave walls, he swept his laser eyes side to side, piercing the smoke and flames, seeking the fatal flaw that crippled every villain, the inevitable chink in Godzilla's scaled armor—

"There!" he shouted. A window, a few feet away, about ten feet up. A way in.

It was a high window in a wall facing Dante's. No smoke or flames spilled out, but shards of broken glass poked up viciously from the bottom sill and reflected the flames that danced around it, veiling the vulnerable opening with false fire. Oh God, even if Glenn or I could reach the window, those jagged shards would slice us to shreds.

But we had no choice. We had to try to reach it, to crawl through to Burt.

Positioning himself below the window, Glenn squatted and laced his fingers together to make a step. I matched him stride for stride, neither one of us explaining the plan, both knowing it, our bleeding friendship inconsequential for the moment. I planted my right boot in his palms. Then he launched me upward with a grunt.

"Can you see anything?" he hollered. Sparks and burning debris rained down around us, plunging past our faces, striking the ground hard. "Can you see him? God, Mona, can you see him?"

I barely uttered the words "I can't reach—" when Glenn screeched and dropped me to the ground. He flumped onto the dirt beside me and rolled, snuffing the small flame that had landed on his shirt. The Dark Knight was no match for Godzilla.

I started to cry. We couldn't reach the window; there was no way to reach Burt. Godzilla was finally devouring the structure he had failed to consume a decade before.

Then I saw it: my Plymouth Knight in shining armor.

Flames reflected off the doorstop's hubcap armor as it wheeled down the street from Dante's like a jousting knight. Then right before my eyes, in one swift movement, the glowing Plymouth Knight seemed to levitate up off its wheeled platform and tilt onto its back, high above the ground. It was now a silver bullet streaking feet-first toward the fire.

Two shadowy figures supported the bullet from below, propelling it forward. Like a million flitting flashlights, the burning embers raining from the sky lit up the hard-set faces of tall Roy and not-so-tall Dad. They were running toward the plant, arms up-stretched, the Plymouth Knight prone across their palms.

Just short of slamming into the wall, Dad and Roy dug in their heels and heaved their arms forward like human catapults. Their roar was primal as they sent the Plymouth Knight forward in its upward path, their shove adding to its momentum, aiming it up and into our window, where it demolished the glass shards and half of the weakened wall in the process. Random debris—wood and stucco, glittering glass and coins, flaming dollar bills and grease-stained burger sacks—filled the air.

Glenn rolled once more to extinguish a second flame on his shirt, but he was back on his feet immediately. His shaggy hair smoked and bloody nicks dotted his face and arms. Even so, he scrambled into position next to the de-capitated wall and laced his fingers again. I stepped into his hand a second time. Roy followed Glenn's lead, hoist-ing Dad, whose red shirt flapped like a cape in the fire's snapping breeze.

The opening was now low enough that Dad and I could climb right in. He went first. But as soon as Super-Mac put a single foot on the weakened edge, the wall disintegrated.

For one brief instant in time, we would-be rescuers were frozen in a tableau: Red-caped Dad was suspended above Roy's head like a bird . . . a plane . . . an angel! And me, soot-blackened, posed like a graceful ice-skater on Glenn's hands. Then the dust from the crumbled wall mushroomed up and swallowed us whole.

Within the cloud, I strained to see. It reminded me of swimming underwater with my eyes open, only feeling smoke wash over my eyeballs was way worse than water. The stinging was intense. But I willed my eyelids wide. My tear ducts ran like faucets, though not enough to drown the fire. I caught glimpses, oh so brief, of the room behind the wall. The Batcave. It was oddly smokeless, more oddly fireless, worst oddly Burtless.

A vortex of fire leaped up between us and the room like an awakened sentry. It was the same vortex I'd seen in the vision with my angel. Only this time, my angel was next to me, wearing a red T-shirt and kicking his way out of a pile of debris instead of emerging from the flames in front of me, swooping in to save the day. This time, no one would be whisking anyone to safety. The only way into the burning building, in to Burt, was blocked.

Rrrrrrrr. . . . The sound of sirens unfroze me.

"Burrrrrrrt!" I yelled, and scrambled to my feet.

My cry was drowned out by Godzilla's roar. A second, involuntary screech crossed my lips as I instinctively flumped to the ground, joining Glenn in another rolling fit of flame snuffing. Then my world exploded in white foam.

The fire retardant, cold and airy, extinguished my burning clothes but left me buried in a pile of sundae-whipped whiteness, my head poking out like the cherry on top. The firefighters had arrived. They were too late, though, to do anything more than contain the fire to this spot, the center of Muessa Junction's campfire ring. The plant was a goner. The rest of the town must be saved.

Behind me, Tuck and firefighters yelled. Margarita screamed about "missing *bebitos*" and "burnt marsh-mallows." My own sobs nearly drowned them all out as a fireman dropped his extinguisher and pulled me to my feet.

The soggy mess of tears, foam, and soot on my face was near blinding, so when I saw the vortex spit out its prize in front of me, I thought I was hallucinating. But I wasn't.

"Burt!"

He was smoky and sizzly and crying like a two-year-old. A haloed shadow lit him from behind like an image from Heaven.

I ripped away from the fireman and threw my arms around the stumbling boy. Just as quickly, the fireman scooped us both up and whisked us away. I'd been wrong about no whisking. I'd been wrong to assume all was lost when it was not. *Mona = ass,* yet again.

Over the fireman's shoulder I saw the vortex lick and ripple and roar, I watched it dissolve into the overall in-ferno. But in the center I saw something, a glimpse of a glimpse, a last look at Burt's haloed shadow. Only, the glowing shadow wasn't attached to Burt now. It existed on its own, shimmery, reflecting the light of the fire as the Plymouth Knight had done just a few moments before.

But it wasn't as solid as the Plymouth Knight; it was more like my vision of Dad in that first fire: fuzzy, vaporous, angelic.

As I watched, Burt's severed shadow seemed to bob and shatter, its atoms dissipating, then dissolving into the fire. But before it disintegrated, it did something strange.

It waved.

It's funny how your mind can play tricks on you. During a crisis, it will tell you one thing, and there's no believing otherwise. But then, once the crisis is over and you replay everything in your head, you question your certainty. You wonder if your mind lied to you. Or if it's lying to you now about lying to you then. Mine lied to me for ten years following the first fire, doling out teasing memories but always withholding the whole story. But with this second fire, I won't doubt. I'll know my mind didn't lie to me, not about this. To my dying day, I'll swear that before it disintegrated, the glowing vision that guided Burt out of this inferno didn't just wave at me . . . it bowed, its palms outstretched like an offering to an empress.

17

The electronic *bing!* announcing my entrance didn't rouse the clerk dozing over his textbook. With two hours more of driving ahead, we needed a pick-me-up, and I figured where better to score that than the sugar-filled aisles of a gas station mini-mart? I started at the refrigerated soda wall in back, then worked my way up and down the aisles. Burnt popcorn and reheated frozen burritos flavored the stale air. A dripping Slurpee machine plip-plopped a blue puddle near the glazed donut rack.

Roy was outside filling the tank of his shiny red Prowler. We were going to raid a place up north, another family-owned burger joint trying to compete with the chains. They'd been all over the news lately for serving up triangular burgers. Customers were driving hundreds of miles just to eat one. It sounded like the perfect place for a raid. And it being Friday, they'd probably have a full house.

A few miles back, Roy and I had parted ways with Pete's Meat Wagon, after caravanning the first leg of our journey. Potter was on a different mission this sunny afternoon. As always, his truck bulged with fatty slabs of cow and pig and crocodile. But today he carried additional cargo: suitcases and sleeping bags in the refrigerated compartment, and Burt, Glenn, and Potter's new girlfriend, Fifi, in the cab. It made for a cramped ride—I could see Fifi's artificial cat whiskers spearing Glenn's shoulder on the turns—but their mood was cheerful when we split. The truck was heading to Boulder, Colorado, home of Fifi's tattoo and piercing parlor, the Cat's Meow, and Potter's new meat route. Along the way, it would deliver Burt and Glenn to the doorstep of one Eugenia Marvella Cruz.

After the fire, Burt's parents were so glad to have him safe and alive—granted, he was missing patches of hair—that they refused to let him anywhere near Uncle Brody's rodeo. I guess they realized that Burt and raging bulls were a recipe for disaster. I could've told them that weeks ago. They rerouted Burt to his great-aunt Eugie instead. After two decades of machete-hacking her way through Third World jungles and digging irrigation ditches with the Peace Corps, eighty-year-old Great-aunt Eugie was no stranger to hard work. That was a good thing, because taming her overeager, overimpulsive great-nephew was going to be a tough assignment. She must have been up for it, though, because she even invited Margarita and Tuck to throw Glenn in as two-for-one, just for the fun of it. I hoped Eugie loved a challenge.

The Glenns jumped at the invitation. Well, Margarita and Tuck jumped. Glenn just caved under the onslaught of Food Wisdom lectures—the one about too many dishonest cooks in a kitchen was pretty effective, but I bet it was the secret-ingredients-just-give-people-gas lecture that finally broke him. Besides, living and homeschooling with Eugie meant he could stay with his new best friend—and get away from his old one.

I knew Glenn and Burt were becoming fast friends before the fire. But in the two weeks after the blaze, they formed a joint at the hip. I saw it, and though it hurt, I think I was starting to understand. Glenn's performance onstage opened my eyes to the fact that he existed as more than just My Friend Glenn. Beginning at InkFest and finishing at Burt's fire, Glenn shed his sidekick costume, no longer the Wonder Boy to my Wonder Woman. He now had his own Boy Wonder.

It was still hard to see him drive off, though, especially since we never said good-bye. But I couldn't face Glenn now any more than he could face me. While I couldn't hold a grudge against a five-year-old boy who'd been too afraid to tell the truth, it was hard not to hold a grudge against a fifteen-year-old boy who couldn't stand up and admit his old mistake. Here I'd thought he had my back all these years. Turns out he was the one sticking a knife in it. Maybe Great-aunt Eugie would help him learn how to stand up and take care of business.

Tuck felt so bad about his complicity in the Great Guy Lie—"It was just for fun and for business; we didn't mean to hurt you, Mona"—that he wanted to go to Great-aunt Eugie's, too. But Margarita, ever practical, convinced him to stay and help her start up and run Tattoo Burger, the newest business venture she'd pulled from her rose-scented sleeve. She saw what was happening around Muessa Junction, and she was determined to take advantage of the turn of events. Flattopped teen burger-flippers were seceding from the chains left and right now, all competing to come up with the most fun takes on fast-food eateries. And Junctioners were responding. Now that they'd had a taste of new and different, new and different was all they wanted. Margarita would combine the Glenns' tattoo reputation with hamburgers and fries, pretty much guaranteeing a bustling business with the over-eighteen demographic in this fast-food-happy town. Margarita knew how to work the Muessa Junction crowd, all right.

She probably had her sites on city hall, truth be told. It was about time this town added a Ms. Mayor to its chain of McMayors.

Before Pete's Meat Wagon had hit the road, Burt had

had one last adventure—with an electric razor. It was my idea, actually. So many large clumps of his black do had been singed in the fire, that, as tiny as he was, he risked being mistaken for a cat with mange and picked up by the Humane Society. So we shaved it bald. Kinda cue ball. Kinda cool. Margarita lectured Potter pretty intensely to nip in the bud any bright ideas he might have about Burt and head tattoos. Her worry was wasted. I doubted Great-aunt Eugie would tolerate such a fashion statement.

Besides, in my mind, the kid's skinned noggin was a statement already. It was a nod to Binny, the nearly bald firefighter who'd saved his life.

Roy and I were the only ones in town who truly believed Burt's story about the rescue. Despite many searches, officials found no evidence of Binny's body in the ashes. They found little of anything, in fact. This time the fire had done its job—there was nothing left on the plant site. Years of people cramming it with old wicker chairs, dead couches, and other random junk had primed the abandoned building for its fated end. That massive pile of tinder had simply awaited its spark.

So Binny's disappearance was officially declared "unsolved" by the same fire chief who'd investigated the first plant fire. I'd believed the chief that first time, but not now. Binny had spent weeks sitting out on the sidewalk talking to smoke, regretting his actions that fateful night ten years ago, and then, after the second fire, there was no sign of him. That alone would've been enough to convince me. But I didn't need those facts to know the truth. And I didn't need Burt's I-swear-on-a-stack-of-Batman-originals story of the glowing vision that guided him through the burning maze, either. I knew the truth because I'd seen it with my own eyes. The bowing vision. Burt's angel. Binny.

Binny had led Burt out of the inferno. Completely unraveled by my fighting with Glenn, the hysterical kid had fled to the secret room in the plant. Once inside, he'd ignited paper after paper, trying to make a full-size torch, eventually succumbing to his Burtness and waving the fire in circles as he imagined a lion tamer would do to keep his beasts under control. But lion tamers know to respect the beast they try to tame—lions are tame only when it suits them. Same with fire. Binny knew that fact well. Glenn was just figuring it out. But Burt had no clue there was even a lesson to learn when he taunted the beast head-on. Clearly, fire taming was not the career for Burt.

By his account, his beast had leaped around the room, lithely, from junk pile to futon to junk pile. Then the ancient, half-burnt timbers joined the flame game, followed by the rest of the shaky structure. Its angry roar sent Burt cowering. Maybe that roar is what Binny heard, what sent him in to Burt's aid.

I wasn't sad, though. My old friend had gotten what he wanted—he conquered the fire, he won. He saved Burt from the lion's jaws and rejoined his soul, all in one swoop. Always my hero, he was now his own. I could almost hear his proud cackle rasping past his grinning lips.

Much like Dad, in fact, who smiled a lot this week, so happy that another child had escaped the flames—and that he had reconnected with me, the daughter he'd pulled from the jaws of that same beast ten years earlier.

Dad still had some spaciness in his eyes, but now I knew why. After I trashed him at the Dumpster that day, he started seeing a therapist. He finally realized he had a reason to get off his futon. The antidepressants they gave him dilated his eyes, but he said he'd rather have them open too wide than not at all. He'd told me all this while we huddled under the firefighters' blankets and watched the plant embers die out. He would have told me sooner if I had come out of my room long enough.

"Mona, I'm sorry," he'd said. "I really didn't know. I was blind to what I'd done to you. Now I'm going to someone who can help me see." It turns out Mrs. Teaburtle was a therapist. Who would've known?

I hadn't said anything when he'd told me. He was right there, sitting next to a fire engine, ready to listen, but I hadn't known what to tell him. I thought about it all that night; I didn't sleep a wink. Then I got up early, climbed out my window, and went to the store. When I got home, I went in through the front door. Dad wasn't sitting by it on a stool. He was in the kitchen, baking cookies. I walked over to him and extended my hands out, palms up. Lying across them like an offering to a king was a game of Chutes and Ladders. Dad smiled, then I did.

He baked cookies nearly every day now, and when I

came home, I went through the front door. I knew he wouldn't be sitting there on a stool, waiting to pounce on me with a bowl of meatballs. He'd be on the futon with a Chutes and Ladders board set up on the floor. Having the board between us made things easy. We could talk about stuff if we wanted, or we could just spin the spinner and move our pawns. It was all about being together. I didn't have to try to keep anyone grounded. I didn't have to control anything. I liked going home now. My house was finally homey.

Dad had something else to look forward to each day, too: leaving the house. When he saw what Roy could do with a few welding tools and some old car parts, he proposed they partner up on a car furniture and futon studio in Binny's abandoned shop. Maybe this would be a job Dad would stick with. He said I was his new muse, so maybe there was some hope after all.

The Society of Cranky Old Fusspots had abandoned all hope, though, as soon as they visited the ashy site. No saving the plant now, historically or otherwise. A cleanup crew was already at work. Soon the site of my infamy would be an empty lot or a park or, if Margarita had her way, the home of the first Tattoo Burger. Frankly, I didn't care one way or the other. Shovel in hand, I'd buried my only remaining interest in the plant.

The night of the burial, Roy had offered to help me, but I declined. Though touched deeply by Roy's new tattoo—a Superman-blue heart that said Forever Friends

on his shoulder, care of Margarita, the queen of hearts—
I'd needed to do this alone. So I stole out to the site one
chilly night, a few days after the fire. The heat wave had
been extinguished with the flames, so I'd had to borrow
an old orange sweatshirt from Tuck. It was XX-huge on
me, but since Muessa Junction stores stocked only shorts
and tank tops, I'd had to take what I could get. I'd also
borrowed a parrot-green ski cap from Roy—quite a match
with my purple hair. But no one was around to suffer the
color clash as I ducked under the yellow police tape and
dug the hole. I'd cried when I shoved the dirt back into the
crater, covering up the sticker resting at the bottom: **BE
THE CHANGE YOU WISH TO SEE IN THE WORLD.** My funeral
tribute to my brave friend, Binny.

Now I was dedicating myself to my poetry raids.
Binny would want that. I'd taken a break from raiding in
the couple of weeks since Binny's fire, so my gig tonight
would be my big postfire coming out. And boy, was I itch-
ing to get out there again. While Roy's art book said not
to rush inspiration, I had no intention of sitting on a futon
for ten years waiting for a muse. I had one, and his name
was Binny. Besides, I felt ready to speak out again. It was
time. But Roy and I still had a couple hundred miles to
cover first.

Inside the mini-mart, I spilled my goods onto the
counter: two bags of Cheetos, a couple of Pepsis, a Ring
Ding, some Cracker Jack, and a withered hot dog
slathered in neon yellow goo. As an afterthought, I

ducked back into the candy aisle and snagged a pack of Bubble Yum, Glenn's favorite. Maybe someday we'd share a pack again. Part of me wondered if that would ever happen, but another part of me had a hunch that Forever Friendships are just that: forever. Maybe they just change a little along the way.

As he rang up my order, the clerk kept looking up at me. He'd scan an item, then look up. Scan, then look up. Scan, then, "Hey, aren't you—"

"Huh?" I blurted. My hand brimmed with coins. He'd interrupted my counting.

"I was just gonna ask, aren't you That Monalisa Kent Girl?"

"Oh," I said. Then I looked my blue eyes into his and smiled warmly. "Yeah, that's me. I'm Monalisa Kent."

"I thought so. I saw you on TV the other day. Pretty cool."

"Thanks."

I paid and turned from the counter, thrusting my arm elbow-deep into the bag. The door *bing*ed at the very moment I tossed a chunk of gum into my mouth. Two points!

Weaving my way among the gas pumps toward Roy, I snapped out a tune. "Twinkle, Twinkle, Little Star."

Or something like it.

about the author

DEBORAH HALVERSON edited children's books for ten years—until she climbed over the desk and tried out the author's chair on the other side. Now she writes books for young readers full-time. Armed with a master's degree in American literature and a fascination with pop culture, she sculpts stories from extreme places and events—tattoo parlors, fast-food joints, and, most extreme of all, high schools. Deborah lives with her husband and triplet sons in San Diego. You can visit her at www.deborahhalverson.com.